SENTIMENTAL JOURNEY

Janet Dailey

CHIVERS

British Library Cataloguing in Publication Data available

Published in 2004 by arrangement with the author

U.K. Hardcover ISBN 0-7540-9924-5
U.K. Softcover ISBN 0-7540-9925-3

The text of this Large Print edition is unabridged.
Other aspects of the book may vary from the original edition.

Set in 16 pt. New Times Roman.

Printed in Great Britain on acid-free paper.

British Library Cataloguing in Publication Data available

Printed and bound in Great Britain by
Antony Rowe Ltd., Chippenham, Wiltshire

Sentimental Journey

Chapter One

Overhead, the sun was bright with the promise of spring. Its direct rays were warming, but the nipping north wind retained the cool breath of winter. A sudden gust whipped dust into an eddy and sent it whirling across the busy intersection, sweeping the street and bouncing off traffic.

Jessica Thorne strolled along the sidewalk, glancing into store windows, her hunter-green coat unbuttoned to the brisk air. She adjusted the shoulder strap of her handbag and slipped her hand back into her coat pocket. The teasing wind mussed the waving wing of silky blond hair at her temple, but Jessica made no attempt to smooth it into place. There would be time enough to freshen up when she returned to the office.

A twinge of restlessness swung her gaze to the Tennessee hills rising around Chattanooga. Evidence of spring was visible in the delicate shading of green on the hillside — new leaves, new grass, new life. Soon the dogwood and rosebud would be blooming. The knowledge shadowed the already dark green of her eyes. But Jessica was unaware of it and would have been at a loss to explain why it should.

Her shoulder brushed against a passerby, returning her attention swiftly to her surroundings. "Excuse me," she murmured in apology, but the woman was already several steps beyond her and didn't hear.

The traffic light at the intersection was green. Jessica quickened her pace to catch the light. As she reached the crosswalk, it turned to amber, Don't Walk flashing beneath it. Traffic surged forward and she had to wait with the other pedestrians on the curb.

A man stood beside her. His imposing height attracted her glance. Coatless against the invigorating weather, he wore a dark business suit and tie. When Jessica would have looked away, the breeze ruffled the sable black mane of hair. A memory clicked in her mind, elusive yet strong.

Her gaze sharpened on his craggy profile. There was a quality of toughness in his lean, hard features that was familiar. Jessica was certain that she knew him, but she couldn't place where or how. He wasn't the kind of man a person could easily forget, which made it all the more confusing.

The man was someone from the past. Time had etched lines around his eyes and mouth, hinting that his age was in the middle thirties. That eliminated the possibility that he was someone she had gone to school with, since she was only twenty-three.

Perhaps the clothing or environment was wrong. The dark suit was hand tailored, the material expensive. He wore it with an ease that indicated that he was accustomed to such clothing, yet Jessica had the distinct feeling he had not been wearing such attire whenever she had met him. What had he worn? A uniform? The answer eluded her.

Becoming aware of her scrutiny, the man glanced at her. His eyes were a shattering blue, narrowed to have the piercing effect of a hard blue diamond. The look was familiar, but Jessica experienced a sense of unease that bordered on fear. She felt her pulse fluttering in alarm. The impulse was strong to look away, to avoid any further contact with the man.

She was stopped from obeying it by the recognition that flickered uncertainly across his face. His raking gaze made a swift, piercing study of her, noting her honey-colored hair and the clouded green of her eyes. So thorough was the inspection that Jessica had the sensation that her coat was stripped away to allow him to examine the slender curves of her figure.

Dark eyebrows drew together in a frown. "Do I know you?"

The voice fitted the man, low pitched and demanding in its curiousness. It struck a familiar chord, but Jessica still could not remember his name.

The shake of her head was more uncertain than negative. "I'm not sure."

"That voice." He paused and seemed to search his memory while his gaze never left her face. "My God!" Recognition glittered in the hard blue eyes, tempered with a hint of skepticism. "Can it be? Jordanna?"

"Jordanna is my sister." Eight years older than Jessica, there was a similarity between the sisters despite the age difference. Besides, all the Thornes had blond hair and either green or blue eyes.

"Of course." His mouth quirked at the corners in self-derisive amusement. "I should have realized you're too young to be Jordanna. You're about the same age Jordanna was when I left. I guess I didn't make allowances for the amount of time that's passed."

Neither noticed the traffic light change, but as the other people at the curb brushed past them to enter the crosswalk, they became aware of the fact. His hand cupped Jessica's elbow to guide her across. The strong, firm grip of his hand sent a tremor of unease through her. The physical contact increased the feeling that she should stay clear of him.

As he escorted her across the intersection, Jessica was still no nearer to remembering who he was. She had searched her memory, trying to recall the men her older sister had dated. None seemed to resemble the man striding beside her.

Stealing a glance at him, Jessica could almost see the wheels turning in his mind. For an instant, there was a cunning look about him. The thought leaped into her mind that, ultimately, he would always get what he wanted. It didn't seem to bode well.

Safely across the street, he stopped, his hand halting her. "What a small world it is!" His lazy smile looked pleased. "Almost my very first day back, I meet a Thorne. It's an amazing coincidence."

"Yes," Jessica agreed, although she didn't know why it was. "Were you a friend of my sister's?"

"A friend?" he repeated with a faintly cynical gleam. "No, I wasn't a friend. I had met your sister, but we never reached the stage of knowing each other well, through no fault of mine."

Jessica was intrigued by his answer. She didn't know what it meant — whether her sister had not wanted to get to know him better or whether her sister was too complicated to know well. She would have pursued the subject, but he changed it.

"Where is Jordanna now? Married, I suppose."

"Yes, she is. She has two children, a boy and a girl. She and her husband live in Florida."

He removed his hand from her arm and Jessica breathed a silent sigh of relief, as if she were once again in full possession of herself. He slipped both hands into the pockets of his slacks, a seeming concession to the brisk air except that his suit jacket was pushed open. The thin material of his shirt covered the muscular wall of his chest down to the trimness of his waist and flat stomach.

When Jessica had first noticed him standing at the crosswalk, there had been an impression of a man on his way somewhere. Now he seemed prepared to stand on the street corner and chat away the day. It was a confusing reversal.

"What about your parents? They're well, I hope," he commented.

Did he know them, too? "Yes. Daddy retired two years ago. They moved to Florida so mother could be near the grandchildren." Jessica wondered if she should be telling him all this. She didn't even know him. Of course, there was a lot he seemed to know already.

"And your brother, did he get his degree from Harvard?" There was something cynical, almost sardonic, in the question.

"Yes. He joined a law firm in Memphis. He's doing quite well." Jessica found herself defending her older brother. She thought she had detected a note of sarcasm when the man had referred to Harvard and it irritated her.

"A Thorne couldn't do any less than very well for himself." The man smiled cruelly when he said it, and behind the joking response, Jessica suspected a taunt. "I never did ask — did Jordanna marry that wealthy Radford man?"

"As a matter of fact, she did, but money had nothing to do with her choice." Jessica bristled.

12

"She happens to love Tom."

"Did I imply otherwise?" He seemed genuinely taken aback by the suggestion. "I apologize for my choice of adjectives to describe Radford. I meant nothing by it."

Was he sincere or merely acting? Jessica couldn't tell. She had been anticipating that he would introduce himself, but obviously he wasn't going to.

"I'm afraid I can't place you." She forced him to make an introduction. "You do look familiar, but. . . ."

"I doubt that we've met before," he said, not at all disconcerted. He withdrew his hand from his pants pocket and offered it to her. "The name is Hayes, Brodie Hayes." His name brought her memory of him into clear focus and a chill shivered down her spine. "You're Jordanna's sister, but I don't know your name."

Shock at his identity had whitened her face. Through the tightness in her throat, she squeezed out the answer, "Jessica."

Automatically she reached to shake his hand. The instant contact was made, warm skin against warm skin, she pulled her hand free.

Brodie Hayes! Her disbelieving eyes swept over the expensive clothes he wore, the fine leather shoes visible beneath the precise crease of his trousers, and the large diamond ring on his finger. Only after these changes were noted did her gaze return to see the bemused and mocking look on his rawly masculine features.

"You do remember me, don't you?" he said.

"I've heard about you." Jessica recovered some of her poise. "I believe I saw you once or twice."

"I vaguely remember that Jordanna had a little sister," Brodie Hayes admitted. "A cute little thing with braces on her teeth."

Jessica didn't smile, nor attempt in any way to reveal the perfect set of white teeth. "You seem to have done very well for yourself, Mr. Hayes," she commented a trifle frigidly.

"Brodie," he corrected, and glanced down at his suit, giving the impression that its cost was of little importance. "I've come a long way from the poor boy who lived on the wrong side of the tracks."

A long way, Jessica agreed silently. He was a rough diamond that had been cut and polished into an expensive gem. But the outer look didn't change the fact that inside he was still that hard, rough diamond capable of cutting through anything.

Finally Jessica obeyed the impulse that had become embedded in her mind from the first moment he had looked at her. "I know I must be keeping you from something important. It was nice seeing you again."

Before she could take a step away, he was speaking. "You're not keeping me from anything." Brodie Hayes disposed of that excuse.

"Surely you must have some old friends you want to look up," she insisted.

"My old friends?" He seemed to consider the idea with bitter regret. "Unfortunately they wouldn't feel comfortable with me anymore. That's one of the prices you pay when you climb the ladder, Jessica. You leave people behind. It isn't often that you can help them come up with you."

"If they're your friends —" Jessica started to protest.

"If you meet someone you haven't seen in years and if that person has made a success of himself while you're still struggling to make ends meet, you get the feeling you're a failure, whether you are or not. It's not a feeling many people want to experience, however much they may like the other person," Brodie reasoned with unquestionable logic and the bitter taste of experience.

"I suppose you're right," she conceded, and glanced pointedly at her watch.

Brodie took the hint. "Am I keeping you from an appointment?"

"I've reached the end of my lunch hour. I have to be back to work in a few minutes." Actually she had plenty of time to spare, but common sense demanded she spend no more time in his company.

"You're a working girl, then, not a lady of leisure." He seemed mildly surprised by the discovery, as if he had expected her parents' wealth was a reason for her to be idle.

"Living the life of leisure can be boring. Per-

15

haps you haven't reached the point where you've discovered that yet." This time it was she who was faintly acerbic in her response.

Brodie Hayes seemed to find it amusing. His mouth remained in its half-curved line, but there was a sparkle of mocking laughter in his hard eyes. It didn't endear him to Jessica.

"Perhaps I haven't," he agreed.

"It was nice seeing you again." She. repeated her earlier exit line with the same result as the last time.

"Have dinner with me this evening," Brodie invited before she could move away. "Your husband is welcome to join us."

"I'm not married," Jessica answered, then realized she had fallen for an old gambit.

"Your boyfriend, then. You do have one?" His skimming look seemed to say any woman as attractive as Jessica had to have a boyfriend or there was something wrong with her.

"Thank you, but I'm afraid I can't accept," she refused as graciously as her clenched jaw would permit, and purposefully adjusted the strap of her shoulder bag.

"Please reconsider." His slow smile was packed with compelling male charm. Jessica was aware of its potency and wavered under its spell. Only a frigid woman could be immune to it, and she was definitely not frigid. "Take pity on a lonely man who's tired of eating his meals by himself."

"If you eat alone, I'm sure it's by choice.

There are probably any number of people who would be delighted to join you." She felt a drawing fascination and fought it vigorously as she discounted his appeal.

"My dinner companions generally want to discuss business or money, directly or indirectly." Brodie Hayes didn't deny her allegation. "Yours is the first remotely familiar face I've seen since I returned. I'm a stranger returning home to find no one here to welcome me. I would like to spend an evening with you, reminiscing about old times."

It was difficult to refuse in the face of his persuasions. He was making her feel guilty and heartless. Only the sensation that he was a little too smooth made Jessica persist in her rejection.

"I doubt if I would be able to do much reminiscing, since your 'old times' were not mine. I would be able to supply you with little information about your contemporaries and where they are and what they're doing today," she argued, hiding her terseness behind a smile.

"My contemporaries were also your sister's and brother's. I'm sure you've heard them speak about their friends." A gust of wind ruffled his midnight black hair. In a careless gesture, his fingers combed it back into order. "You'd probably be surprised at how much information you've unconsciously gathered."

"Possibly," she conceded that he might be right.

"Shall I pick you up at eight o'clock?" Brodie didn't repeat his invitation, but rephrased it to take her acceptance for granted.

Jessica hesitated, finding herself at a loss to battle him with words. With a sigh, she released the breath she had unconsciously been holding and flashed him a quick smile.

"Eight o'clock will be fine," she agreed, and glanced at her watch. "I have to run. See you tonight . . . Brodie." Her tongue tripped over his given name.

"Tonight," he agreed with an arrogantly pleased smile.

But Jessica was already moving away, not allowing him another chance to detain her. She hurried down the sidewalk, not looking behind her to see if Brodie Hayes was watching her leave.

There was no sense of triumph in having eluded him, nor in having bested him. She had agreed to the dinner invitation for the simple reason that it was the easy way out. She knew she wouldn't be going with him when she had accepted. Not because she was going elsewhere that evening. The fact was that Brodie Hayes did not know where she lived, and her telephone was not listed in the directory, so there was no chance he could find her. A man like Brodie Hayes would not take kindly to being stood up, but with luck she would never bump into him again.

At the building where she worked, Jessica

paused to glance behind her. She scanned the people on the sidewalk and felt silly for thinking that Brodie might have followed her. With an impatient shake of her head, she pushed open the glass door and walked in.

Riding the elevator, Jessica shrugged out of her coat and tried not to let her mind dwell on what she had just done. But it had left a sour aftertaste in her mouth. Her expression was downcast and slightly preoccupied as she entered the outer office area.

Ann Morrow, the receptionist, glanced up and frowned. "I wasn't expecting you for another twenty minutes, Miss Thorne."

"I came back early," she answered abruptly, and immediately tempered her sharpness. "I wanted to look over the Atkins account."

"I took the file into Mr. Dane's office a few minutes ago." The girl lifted her shoulders in mute apology.

"That's all right." Jessica hadn't really been interested in looking over the account, at least not overly so. Now that her uncle, Ralph Dane, was going over the file, there was no point her looking at it. "I'll be in my office if anyone calls for me."

As Jessica turned away, she found herself thinking that Brodie Hayes wouldn't call. He didn't know where she worked, either.

A door opened and a tall, distinguished-looking man came striding out. His dark hair was grayed at the temples, a pair of dark-rimmed glasses were in his hand.

"Ann . . ." he began, glancing up from the file he held. At the familiar sound of her uncle's voice, Jessica paused instinctively. His peripheral vision caught her presence and his attention immediately shifted to her. "Jessie, you're back already. You're just the person I wanted to see. Come into my office."

He didn't wait to see if she was coming as he retraced his path, leaving the door to his private office open for her. Jessica hesitated for only a split second, then tossed her coat over the back of the chair beside the receptionist's desk and followed him. Closing the door, she walked to a leather-covered chair and set her bag on the seat.

"Back early from lunch, aren't you?" he accused in his terse, clipped voice. "Not that I mind. This Atkins account is a shambles." He dropped the file on his desk and pushed back the cuff of his jacket to glance at his watch. "What are you — a glutton for work? Twenty minutes early."

"I had my lunch. There wasn't any shopping I wanted to do, so I came back to the office." Jessica shrugged.

"No shopping, huh?" Ralph Dane grunted. "I'd celebrate the day your Aunt Rebecca ever said that!" Hitching up his trousers, he sat down in the swivel chair behind his desk and opened the file holder. "I've just looked over the Atkins file. The ad campaign is . . . hokey,

20

for want of a better word. Parts of it are worth saving, but this. . . ."

A red pencil began slashing out lines of copy while Jessica moved closer to the desk, turning at an angle to see what he was eliminating. Her concentration held for two minutes until the words "success" and "hometown boy" made her attention stray. They came too soon after her encounter with Brodie Hayes for her not to apply them to him instead of this old and valued account.

"Are you listening to me, Jessie?" her uncle demanded impatiently.

She winced, both at her inattention and his diminutive use of her name. "Sorry, I was thinking," she admitted.

"Not about this, obviously." He flipped the pencil onto the desk top and leaned back in his chair, folding his hands in his lap. "Out with whatever it is that's on your mind so we can concentrate on this."

"It wasn't anything important."

"Important enough for you not to pay attention. Get it off your chest," he ordered.

Jessica knew her uncle well enough to know he would persist with his questions until she came up with a response. She had never been any good at making up stories, so she settled for the truth, or a portion thereof.

"On my way back to the office, I met a man who lived here several years ago, a hometown boy who's doing quite well now. The comparison with the Atkins campaign clicked in my mind."

"Who is he?"

"Brodie Hayes." Jessica was surprised by how naturally she spoke his name.

"Never heard of him," her uncle grumped. "Anything else?"

"No." Nothing that she was going to tell him.

The trick she had pulled on Brodie Hayes was strictly private. It wasn't something she was proud of and she wasn't going to confide in her uncle. Despite their family relation he was still her boss, and she didn't want him to know she had used devious means to handle a situation. He was too open and aboveboard in his dealings to condone such behavior.

"Take this file, look over my notes, add some of your own, and take it back to the boys. Tell them they'd better come up with something better than this or they're fired." He closed the folder and handed it to her.

Hiding a smile at his false threat, she nodded. "Will do."

In the outer office, she paused to pick up her coat. Ann Morrow was on the telephone. Jessica pointed to her office to indicate to the receptionist that that was where she would be, and the girl nodded.

Her office was small, containing no more than a desk, two chairs and a filing cabinet, but then she was a very junior member of the staff. Jessica's first year with her uncle's advertising firm had been spent in the back room, learning the fundamentals. When her apprenticeship had been served, she had been elevated to handling accounts.

In truth, the accounts were with old established customers, and Ralph Dane worked closely with her on these. Jessica knew she had obtained the job because she was his niece. But she also knew that if she weren't capable, the family ties would not guarantee that she would keep the job.

Sighing, Jessica settled into the lumpy seat of her chair and opened the file. She skimmed over the cuts and read the notes in the margin. Some of the changes she would have made; others she wouldn't have noticed. Her uncle had an instinctive knack for what was abrasive to the public. Perhaps she would learn this talent in time.

In time. Time. How long had it been since she had last seen Brodie Hayes? Ten years? She had been — what . . . eleven or twelve?

Chapter Two

Jessica decided she had been eleven years old. It was surprising what an indelible impression Brodie Hayes had made on her. She could even recall vividly the first time she had heard his name. It had been on a Saturday afternoon in July. She had been in the family room with her sister and brother, listening to the stereo.

Despite the vast age difference, they had never minded Jessica hanging around them. Her adoration of them had bordered on hero worship. They were so much older, had done so much more and were permitted to do so much more that Jessica got a vicarious thrill out of quietly listening to them talk.

Her father had walked in and raised his voice to be heard over the volume of the music. "Jordanna, there's a rather disreputable-looking man at the front door who wants to speak to you."

At first, her sister had only expressed mild surprise that someone was calling to see her, but as her father's words had sunk in, her expression changed to one of apprehension and dismay.

"It couldn't be," she protested. "Brodie Hayes wouldn't come here."

"Brodie Hayes?" Her brother, Justin, frowned

in surprise. "You never mentioned that you were seeing him."

"I'm not," Jordanna protested, while Jessica looked on with mounting interest. Her brother had sounded angry and faintly outraged. It made Jessica wonder who this Brodie Hayes was. "A bunch of us went swimming at the lake a couple of weeks ago," Jordanna explained in defense of her brother's accusation. "Brodie was there. I talked to him, just to be polite, and he's been pestering me to go out with him ever since."

"He's no good, Jordanna," Justin stated flatly. "Stay away from him."

"I intend to." Jordanna was emphatic. "There's something about him that scares me."

"If you feel that way, Jordanna," her father spoke up, "I'll tell him that you don't want to see him."

Jessica sat quietly on the large, boldly colored rug in front of the fireplace, glancing from one speaker to another, her head turning back and forth as if she were watching a tennis match. With every word that was spoken, her ears had figuratively grown bigger and bigger.

For Jordanna who was so self-possessed and so popular to be frightened of anyone seemed beyond Jessica's ken. And Justin's warning added to her wide-eyed intrigue.

"No, dad." Jordanna hesitated before refusing the offer. "I'll talk to him."

But, by her expression, Jessica could tell that

her sister wasn't looking forward to it as she left the room. Justin then walked over to turn the volume of the stereo down to low. Jessica had the impression that he expected their sister to call for help and he wanted to be sure to hear her.

Her father remained in the room. Turning to Justin, he demanded, "Just who is this Brodie Hayes?"

Justin appeared to hesitate, a frown permanently implanted on his forehead. "He was in my class in high school — that is, when he bothered to come to class. He was smart, though. He wasn't in school half the time and still managed to pull above-average grades. But he dropped out when he was sixteen. He runs with a rough crowd. Those who haven't been in reform school have seen the inside of a jail cell."

"I don't like the idea of Jordanna getting mixed up with that sort." Her father's expression deepened with concern. He took a step toward the door. "I think I'd better send that young man on his way."

"No, dad, let Jordanna handle it," Justin insisted. "Believe me, it's better that Brodie doesn't develop a grudge against the Thorne family."

Her father looked grim, but did not argue. Neither man had been paying any attention to the silent Jessica. Silently she slipped from the room and darted up the open staircase to her bedroom. The reason was simple and obvious: from the window of her room, she was able to overlook and overhear what was going on below.

Her first glimpse of Brodie Hayes fulfilled all the expectations her vivid imagination had conjured up. Coal black hair, black as the devil's, gleamed in the sunlight. Tall, with a powerful physique, he dwarfed her slightly built sister. Faded jeans showed signs of excessive wear. His bare arms were corded with sinewy muscles. He was surrounded by an aura of toughness that was doubly intimidating to Jessica when coupled with what her brother had said about him.

Jordanna appeared on the surface to be composed, but Jessica who knew her well saw the nervous trembling of her smile and the distance her sister tried to maintain from the rough-looking, dark-haired man. From her lofty perch Jessica eavesdropped on the conversation.

"Are you engaged?" Brodie Hayes demanded.

"No," Jordanna answered defensively.

"Are you going steady with anyone?" He had taken a step closer and Jessica trembled in sympathy for her sister.

"Not at the present time, I'm not," Jordanna admitted in a tone that indicated that that fact was of little importance.

"Then I don't see what's stopping you from

accepting my invitation." It was more than a challenge.

"I'm sorry." Jordanna walked several feet away, escaping from the intimidation of his closeness. "I've already told you I'm busy. I'm sorry you've come all this way for nothing, but you should have called first."

"Yeah," he agreed cynically, "all the way from the wrong side of town."

The remark seemed to make Jordanna uneasy. "I said I was sorry, Brodie."

"And I'm supposed to say it's all right. Forget it." The mockery in his voice was harsh. He took a deep breath, the muscled wall of his chest expanding to strain the few buttons of his shirt that were fastened. "Very well, consider it said. But there's one other thing; I haven't given up." Peering from her window, Jessica shivered with fear because it had sounded like a warning. "You have more class in your little finger, Jordanna, than all the other girls I know put together. I'll be seeing you again, you can bet on it."

On that ominous note, he turned and started down the long sidewalk to the driveway. Jessica heard the closing of the front door, indicating that her sister had reentered the house, but she wasn't able to take her eyes off the tall, dark-haired man striding away.

There was something about the way he moved, lithe and supple, that reminded her of a wild animal. She remembered the sensation she

28

had felt when her parents had taken her to a zoo in California and she had seen a large wolf loping across an enclosure designed to resemble his native habitat. She had sensed she was looking at something ruthless, predatory and dangerous.

Staring after Brodie Hayes, Jessica had the same feeling. And as with the wild lobo, she experienced the same compelling fascination to watch Brodie Hayes from a safe distance. But she knew that if she ever met him face to face, she would be terrified.

Her knees were shaking when he drove away in a battered Chevrolet. Part of her wanted to curl up in the big, overstuffed chair in her room until the trembling stopped. But the stronger urge was to race downstairs to discover her sister's reaction to the meeting.

It was as easy to slip, unseen, into the family room as it had been to slip out. Her sister was standing at a window, staring at the expansive rear lawn, and Justin was watching her. There was no sign of their father.

"You should have told him you didn't want to see him again," Justin said with undisguised impatience.

"That's easier said than done. And I doubt if he would have listened." Jordanna moved away from the window and began nibbling on a fingernail. "God, do you know what he told me, Justin?" She laughed, but it had been a shrill sound. "That I had more class in my little finger than all the girls he knew!"

"That isn't surprising, considering the kind of girls he knows. You know the reputation the girls have that he dates. If you were ever seen with him, people would say the same thing about you."

Jessica checked herself just in time from asking what people would say. That wasn't the moment to interrupt the conversation with questions. She kept silent and played the little mouse in the corner.

"I know that. Believe me, I have no intention of going anywhere with him," Jordanna stated emphatically.

"I should hope not!"

Jordanna shuddered and rubbed her arms. "There's something about him that frightens me. I think it's his eyes — they're so piercing. You have the feeling he's looking into your soul. And they never seem to register any emotion. Even when he smiles, his eyes don't."

"What color are his eyes?" Jessica had piped up, forgetting her vow to remain silent.

"Blue," Jordanna answered automatically, then exchanged a quick glance with Justin as they both realized she had been listening.

Since her presence had been noted, Jessica tried to include herself in the discussion. "I thought he looked dangerous," she added.

"When have you ever seen him?" Jordanna frowned.

But Justin smiled. "I'll bet it was from your

bedroom window, wasn't it, Jessica?"

"I wanted to see what he looked like," she answered in defense of her action.

"You shouldn't spy on people like that." The admonishment came from her sister.

"What's the matter?" Justin teased. "Afraid of what little sister might see when you and Tom say your good-nights?"

"Oooh!" Jordanna picked up a pillow from the sofa and threw it at her brother.

Much to Jessica's regret, the conversation never got back to Brodie Hayes. She knew it was because she was there.

The second time Jessica had seen Brodie Hayes, she and her sister had been in the house alone. Justin was off playing tennis with some of his buddies. Their father was working and their mother was at a committee meeting of the local auxiliary.

Skinny and shapeless in her bathing suit, Jessica was swimming in the pool in the backyard. Just as she entered the house through the rear sliding glass doors, the bell at the front door rang.

"I'll answer it!" she shouted, and raced barefoot to the entryway.

With the abandonment of a young person, she flung open the front door. Instantly the smile of greeting died as a shaft of cold fear rooted her to the ground. Her hand continued to clutch the doorknob. On the threshold stood Brodie Hayes with his black hair and cool blue eyes.

"Is Jordanna home?"

To Jessica, it seemed more like a demand than a question. Fear had a stranglehold on her vocal cords and she wasn't able to utter a sound. Brodie Hayes took her silence and the fact that the door was opened so wide as permission to enter.

Her heart was pounding so hard, she thought it would explode as he stepped into the foyer. She watched his gaze make a sweeping arc of the interior of the house. She wanted to run, but as if she were in a nightmare, her legs were paralyzed.

"Who was at the door, sis?" Jordanna's voice called from another room.

Jessica wanted to scream a warning, but not a sound came from her throat. She heard her sister walking toward the entryway and noted the way Brodie had turned to face the sound. Inside, she was crying for being so frightened. She could have told him Jordanna wasn't home if only she hadn't been so terrified.

It was too late when the footsteps stopped and Brodie said, "Hello, Jordanna." And Jessica noticed that his eyes didn't mirror the smile parting his mouth.

There were more footsteps. Jessica nearly jumped out of her skin when her sister's hand touched her shoulder, and she looked up into the nervous smile of her sister. Her cloudy green eyes were rounded in apology and Jordanna's hand tightened in reassurance.

"You'd better go up to your room and change out of that wet swimsuit." Her sister provided her with an excuse to escape.

The touch of Jordanna's hand broke the grip of paralysis. Jessica raced up the stairs two at a time, but she went no farther than the top. There she huddled against the wall to listen, shaking like a leaf.

"I happened to be in the neighborhood," Jessica heard Brodie say, "and thought I'd drop by to see if you'd like to go for a ride. It's a beautiful afternoon."

"I'm sorry you made another wasted trip. I can't go with you," Jordanna refused, then hurried an explanation. "There wouldn't be anyone here to stay with my little sister. I couldn't leave her alone."

Hiding at the top of the stairs, Jessica cringed. She didn't think her sister should tell him they were alone. What if he decided to rob them?

"How old is your sister?" Brodie Hayes asked. "Nine? Ten?"

"She's eleven."

"Then she's old enough to stay by herself. Nobody's hung around to look after me since I was eight."

"That doesn't matter," Jordanna insisted. "We don't do that. Besides, Jessica is a girl, so it's different."

"Then you won't change your mind and come for a ride with me?" He sounded as if he expected a negative answer.

"I can't. I've already explained that I have to stay here."

"In that case, I'll stay and keep you company."

At his statement, Jessica breathed in sharply. Alarm trembled through her, bones knocking together so loudly that she was sure they could hear her in the foyer below.

"I'm sorry, but I'll have to ask you to leave, Brodie. Our parents don't allow us to have friends in unless one of them is here, as well," Jordanna explained, quite bravely, Jessica thought.

"Do you always do what your parents tell you?" He seemed to be mocking Jordanna's strict adherence to her parents' wishes.

"My parents don't make unreasonable requests." Jordanna didn't say any more in defense of her parents or her stand.

"If I come back later this afternoon, when your mother or father are home, would you come out with me then?"

Jessica held her breath, knowing her sister was going to refuse, yet wondering what excuse she could make for not going with him.

Jordanna's answer, when it came, was straightforward, her voice slightly breathy. "No."

"Why?" Despite the quiet, even pitch of his voice, it contained the threatening ring of challenge. Upstairs, Jessica quivered as an eternity of seconds ticked away in silence. "Are you afraid of being seen with me?" His voice was so controlled, so lacking in emotion that it sent chills down Jessica's spine and she was able to imagine how her sister felt, "Or are you just afraid of me?"

"It's nothing like that, Brodie," Jordanna hastened to assure him.

"If it isn't where I live or what you think I am, would you mind telling me why you keep turning me down?" A thread of cynicism had been sown through his voice, skeptical and taunting.

"Because —" Jordanna paused for a fraction of a second before completing her answer "— I'm not interested in seeing you. There's someone else . . . that I like."

"Radford," Brodie Hayes concluded. "Your parents would approve of him. But they would never welcome me into their home, would they?"

"I wouldn't know." Her sister's voice contained a faintly haughty air. "The question has never arisen."

"Probably because everyone knows the answer."

"That isn't fair," Jordanna protested.

"Fair?" Brodie Hayes repeated in a laughing sound. "At least I know where I stand with you . . . and why," he added in a voice that indicated he'd drawn his own conclusion. "Would you like to know where you stand with me?"

That apprehensive note made Jessica peep around the wall. Her eyes rounded in fear when she saw her sister flattened against the wall, Brodie's arms on either side, caging her there. Afraid of what he might be planning to do to Jordanna, she rose to clutch the banister. He leaned intimidatingly close, all but blocking her sister from Jessica's view.

"Brodie, please —" he had made a harsh mockery out of her words. "Please, what? Please, get lost?" Jordanna made no response, holding her ground and meeting his look. "Okay, if that's what you want." He pushed away from the wall. "I guess I just stepped out of my class, didn't I?" Jordanna opened her mouth to say something. "Don't bother, I can show myself out. Unless you would prefer that I leave by the back door."

"No, I —"

But Brodie didn't give her sister a chance to complete the sentence, turning and walking to the front door with swift yet unhurried strides.

When the door closed, Jessica sped down the stairs, racing toward her sister. "Are you all right, Jordanna? I was so scared!"

"Jessica!" Her sister caught her by the shoulders and looked at her in surprise. "I thought you were in your room."

"I waited at the top of the stairs," she admitted. "I didn't think you'd be able to send him away. I thought he might hurt you."

36

"You have much too vivid an imagination," Jordanna sighed.

"I saw him," Jessica protested. "He'd backed you up to the wall. I just know he was going to do something."

"He was just trying to scare me a little because I hurt his pride by refusing to go out with him. But he didn't do anything, Jessica. You see, I'm all right." Jordanna smiled brightly. "Now go on upstairs and change out of your swimsuit. Mom would have fits if she caught you around the house in that wet thing."

Jessica obeyed, but she wasn't convinced that her fears for her older sister had been groundless. She had never forgotten the scene nor the sense of peril she had experienced licking through her veins.

Three weeks later she had seen Brodie Hayes for the third time, and the last time until today. As before, the doorbell had rung and Jessica had raced to answer it. Part of it was almost a replay of the previous time. She had stopped short at the sight of Brodie Hayes.

"Is your sister home?" he asked.

Robbed of speech by the memory of the other scene, Jessica shook her head. Jordanna had gone out with some friends for the afternoon.

"Do you know when she'll be back?"

Again her head moved swiftly from side to side. If she had known, she would never have told him. As it was, she didn't have to lie.

"Would you give her a message?"

This time her head bobbed in agreement.

His mouth quirked at the action. "Can't you talk, kid?"

The taunt stung Jessica into speech. "I can talk."

"So that's your problem, a mouthful of metal." As soon as he spoke, Jessica pressed her lips tightly together to hide the braces he had seen. "Tell Jordanna that I stopped to tell her goodbye. I'm leaving town." Jessica nodded and Brodie Hayes started to turn away. Then he hesitated, his piercing blue eyes glancing back at her. "And tell her when I do come back, I won't be out of her class."

He walked away. Jessica couldn't remember his name ever being mentioned after that, not coupled with success or failure.

His statement on that long-ago yesterday echoed clearly in her mind. On the surface, he seemed to have succeeded. That proud chip on his shoulder hadn't been in evidence, unless it had been hidden by the superb cut of his suit. But why had he come back? After all this time, what had he hoped to find? Jessica shook her head, not finding any logical answer.

It was nothing to her. He was nothing to her, except part of an incident in her childhood, one that had probably been dramatized out of proportion by her imaginative age. It was only by sheer chance she had seen him again. The odds didn't favor a repeat, so she attempted to push all the memories, past and present, to the back of her mind.

As the rest of the afternoon progressed, it became easier. The Atkins account demanded her attention; conferring with the artists and admen in the larger office to come up with a more palatable campaign.

It was after five before she finally left the office for her apartment. It was a spacious, two-bedroom affair, much larger than she really needed. The spare bedroom had been used often by her family, since they were all known to drop in without warning for a visit. Justin had stayed with her while on a business trip as recently as a month ago.

Entering the apartment, Jessica deposited her bag and the mail on the coffee table in the living room and opened the gold-flowered drapes concealing the sliding glass doors to a small balcony. In a pattern that had become routine, she continued to her bedroom. There she changed out of the vested camel tan skirt and blouse into a pair of becoming mint-green slacks with a matching silk blouse in a blue and green design.

On her way back to the living room she stopped in the kitchen for a glass of chocolate milk, then continued to the gold sofa to read the day's mail. It was her time of the day to relax and unwind from the pressures of the office.

In the mail, there was a letter from her

mother filled with news of her grandchildren — Jessica's niece and nephew. Normally Jessica would have read the letter through at least twice, but this night she put it aside after one reading and picked up a women's magazine, choosing to immerse herself in an excerpt from a best-selling novel instead.

Chapter Three

As engrossing as the story had turned out to be, Jessica found it impossible to ignore the empty rumblings of her stomach. She turned the corner of the page and set the magazine aside. Paying no attention to the chiming of the clock, she walked into the kitchen. A plate of cold chicken and a macaroni salad were in the refrigerator. She set them on the breakfast bar and walked to the cutlery drawer of the kitchen cabinets.

The buzzer at the door to her apartment interrupted her, and she frowned and searched her mind for who it might be. The No Soliciting sign usually kept the door-to-door salesmen at bay. Her friends generally telephoned before coming over. Shrugging that guessing served no purpose, Jessica entered the living room and crossed to the door.

Opening it, she was carried back to that long-ago yesterday, and her hand froze on the doorknob. Shock struck the words from her throat. She could only stare at Brodie Hayes.

A half smile touched his hard mouth, but he seemed oblivious to her surprise. The clear blue of his eyes and the jet black of his hair was intensified by the sweater he wore, the pale color of smoke, and charcoal gray slacks. Hard and smooth as a diamond, he was a compelling figure, all male, totally at ease.

Leaning a hand against the door jamb, he eyed her somewhat mockingly. "How did you know that I planned for us to have a very informal dinner this evening? Can you read minds, Jessica?"

The shock receded into astonishment. "How did you know where I lived?" she breathed incredulously.

"I called your office and explained to your uncle that we were having dinner together tonight, but that you'd forgotten to give me your new address. He was kind enough to provide me with it." His answer did not hold any underlying tone of mockery, as if he genuinely believed the omission of her address had been an oversight.

"But —" it was too much for Jessica to take in "— how did you know where I worked?"

"Simple deduction." Brodie straightened and stepped over the threshold, forcing her backward into the living room. "I couldn't believe that a Thorne would be left entirely on her own. There had to be some member of the family who would be in frequent contact with you. Luckily for me I remembered your uncle owned an advertising agency."

"Yes, it was lucky, wasn't it?" Jessica was breathing unevenly, not quite sure that he believed what he said. "If you hadn't remembered, we both would be dining alone tonight."

"Something neither of us would have enjoyed, isn't that right?" For all the smoothness of his response, there was the barest trace of a challenge in his voice.

It was the first indication that perhaps he believed she had not given her address on purpose. But Jessica couldn't be certain. At this point, it would be ill mannered to admit it. It was imperative that she somehow conceal the truth.

Some of her poise had returned, but her pulse had not yet regained its normal rate. Turning away from him, she nervously licked her lips and made up a story in her mind.

"I don't know what possessed me to overlook such a vital thing as my address." She laughed stiffly. "I didn't realize it until I was back in my office, and by then it was too late. And I didn't know where to reach you."

On the last word, she turned to face him, lifting her hands in a gesture that indicated there had been nothing she could do. The half smile remained in place, the blue eyes unblinking and bland.

"You could have checked the hotels. There aren't that many of them in Chattanooga," Brodie pointed out. Dark lashes lowered to screen the blue eyes as he shrugged. "I'd forgotten. A Thorne wouldn't call various hotels searching for a man."

Jessica almost breathed her sigh of relief aloud. "It would have been awkward. But I wasn't even sure if you were staying in a hotel."

"And you didn't check," he said with faint accusation.

"No, I didn't check," Jessica admitted quite freely. "Do you blame me?" she countered. "I barely know you."

"I don't blame you at all. If the roles were reversed, I might feel the same mixture of regret and indifference." He released her gaze and glanced at the walnut-cased mantel clock. "Have you eaten yet?"

Should she lie and claim she had eaten? Jessica toyed with the thought. But she was hungry and the growling of her stomach would tell him she was lying. His sharp gaze was back on her, waiting for an answer.

"As a matter of fact, I was just fixing myself something when the doorbell rang," she admitted. "So I haven't eaten."

"Good, then we'll be able to have dinner together." His eyes briefly noted the blouse and slacks she wore. "There's no need to change. Where we're going, anything else would be out of place. If you're ready to leave, we can go now."

"Give me a couple of minutes to put away the food in the kitchen," she asked as he inclined his head in silent agreement.

Her hands were shaking as she set the chicken and salad back in the refrigerator, and she took a deep breath and tried to calm her rattled senses. She would get through the evening somehow without letting him see how his company affected her, she vowed to herself.

"Ready?" A dark brow lifted when she reentered the living room.

"Yes." Jessica took her bag from the coffee table and slipped the long strap over her shoulder.

Brodie held the door open for her and waited in the hallway while she locked the dead bolt. Side by side, they walked outdoors. His hand came up to rest on her backbone above her waist. Its guiding pressure was light, but sufficient for Jessica to be aware of the contact and to be unnerved by it. He directed her to a dark blue Cadillac parked at the curb, unlocked the passenger door for her and helped her in.

When Brodie slid behind the wheel, Jessica ran her hand over the cream velour armrest. "It's a beautiful car," she said to break a silence that, to her, had become uneasy.

A smile twitched at the corners of his hard mouth. "I'll tell the rental agency you said so." He slid the key in the ignition and started the engine.

"It isn't yours, then?" Somehow she hadn't expected that answer.

"Not this one." Which indicated that he owned one. As he turned the car into the street, his gaze skipped to her. "I always dreamed of owning a Cadillac. Most poor kids do. As soon as I could afford it, it was one of the first things I bought. Now it's stored in a garage somewhere." He was incredibly indifferent to the fact.

Jessica stared. She couldn't help it. "You do know where it's stored, don't you?"

"In Louisville, I think." His attention was on the traffic. His reply was so absently given that Jessica had to believe he wasn't certain of its location and wasn't bothered that he didn't know. "That sounded arrogant, didn't it?" Brodie shot her a brief, self-mocking glance. "Since I travel a great deal, it hasn't been practical to have my personal car wherever I am for a very long time. I've taken the fact for granted without realizing how it might sound to someone else."

"How did your travels bring you to Chattanooga after all these years?" Jessica questioned. "You never did mention this noon why you were back."

"It was a combination of circumstances," Brodie said, which told her absolutely nothing. "Mostly it's a sentimental journey to see where it all began." Again she was the cynosure of his blue eyes. "You find that hard to believe, don't you, Jessica?" he said, seemingly with the ability to read her mind. "But it's difficult to know where you are if you've forgotten where you came from."

"So you're taking a trip into the past, so to speak." She thought she understood. At the same time, she was also discovering that Brodie was a complicated man with many

46

facets like a well-cut gem.

"Tonight's journey brings me here." He swung the long car into the partially lighted parking lot of a restaurant. "Have you eaten here before?"

It was a nondescript building with a pink neon sign spelling out the word restaurant. It was a busy place as evidenced by the numerous other vehicles parked in the lot and the crowded tables visible through the windows.

"I'm not sure," Jessica admitted.

"It isn't surprising if you haven't." His remark seemed to be a sardonic comment on her more prosperous background. The engine was turned off, but Brodie made no attempt to get out of the car. Instead he gazed at the building, alive with sounds and people. "When I was a boy, my father brought me here every Friday, payday. It was a weekly treat, the one night we ate out. As I grew older, it was a place to hang out with my friends. I checked earlier this afternoon to see if it was still in business, but I can't vouch for the food. Are you game to try it?" His look held a hint of challenge.

Jessica wondered if he thought she was going to become snobbish and indicate that the place wasn't good enough for her. If he did, he didn't know her very well.

"Why not? All those people can't be wrong." She glanced at the filled tables inside.

Brodie opened his door and stepped out. Jessica didn't wait for him to walk around the

47

car and open her door. She did it herself instead and joined him at the front of the car, to walk to the restaurant entrance.

"I have another confession to make," Brodie said as they wound their way through the tables to an empty booth against the wall.

"What's that?" Jessica slid onto the bench seat.

He sat opposite her. "This is also where I brought my dates, especially the more beautiful ones, so I could show off in front of the guys." He was smiling as he answered, a mocking glint in his eyes.

But she didn't return the smile. "Is this where you would have brought Jordanna if she'd agreed to go out with you?"

"More than likely." Brodie nodded, his gaze narrowing fractionally.

"Are you fulfilling a fantasy, bringing me here as a stand-in for my sister?"

"Probably," he admitted.

Jessica was certain the truth was more positive than his answer. A waitress brought them menus, and Jessica opened hers and began studying it. The fare ran the full gamut from sandwiches to salads to full-course meals, breakfasts and desserts. She hadn't made up her mind when the waitress returned.

"Have you decided?" Brodie asked.

"Not yet." She didn't glance up from the menu. "Go ahead and order."

"As I remember, the most popular item on

the menu was a hamburger, french fries and a malt. I'll have that. Coffee instead of the malt," he told the waitress.

Jessica closed the menu. "I'll have the same, with the malt, chocolate."

When the waitress moved away, Brodie said, "You didn't have to order that."

"I happen to like hamburgers and french fries," she defended her choice.

"I remember times when I had to wait for my date to order so I would know whether I could afford to have anything. It was always a nightmare wondering if some girl was going to order an expensive steak and if I had enough money to pay for it." His mouth quirked into a dry half smile. "At sixteen, I didn't know what Chateaubriand was, let alone how to pronounce it." He opened a flat cigarette case and offered it to Jessica. "Cigarette?"

"Thank you." She took one and bent her head to the gold lighter in his hand. A yellow flame curled around the tip of the cigarette and Jessica leaned back, blowing a stream of smoke into the air. She watched Brodie light his own cigarette, noting the expensive gold lighter. "That's a far cry from penny matchbooks."

"What would you know about penny matchbooks?" Brodie mocked cynically.

"A lot of firms use matchbooks for advertisement. It's my job to know the cost of such items." She didn't claim more intimate knowledge than that.

"What's your position with the agency?"

Jessica sensed an implication that her job was a superfluous one. "Uncle Ralph doesn't practice nepotism, if that's what you're thinking," she told him firmly. "True, he did offer me the job because I was his niece, but if I'm not any good, he isn't going to keep me."

"No businessman would be successful if he didn't have that attitude." Brodie neither admitted nor denied that her correction was justified as he repeated his question. "What do you do?"

"I handle the older, more established accounts so I can gain experience before attempting to solicit new accounts," she said, and resented the way he made her feel so defensive.

"Your uncle is missing a bet. If you came into my office with a proposal, I would have a great deal of difficulty looking at you and turning it down."

His look was suddenly very male and very suggestive. Jessica flamed under it and changed the subject to hide the hot confusion rushing through her.

"What do you do? You didn't say earlier."

"I take things that are broken or run-down, repair them and make them run smoothly again." He flipped the ash from his cigarette into the metal ashtray that was blackened by previous smokes.

"What kind of things?" she asked curiously.

"Companies, mostly manufacturing firms."

"So now you own a whole string of successful companies," Jessica concluded.

"No. I buy controlling interest in a faltering company, make it successful again, then sell it for a handy profit."

"What did you do? Go back to school and take a business-management course?"

"No. A long time ago I learned that ninety percent of everything you need to know in life is common sense. The other ten percent I could buy." Brodie studied the smoke curling from the tip of his cigarette, half-burned down. "I was irritated and impatient with school. You learned all the subjects and no one taught you how to apply them in life."

"Is that why you quit?" Jessica wanted to know.

"I quit because I thought I was smart. Later, I didn't go back because I didn't want to find out how ignorant I was. Over the years, I've had to educate myself, but it wasn't easy," he stated.

Unwillingly Jessica felt a glimmer of admiration. Nothing he had said resembled bragging or boasting, just a simple statement of facts. She suspected he was as hard on himself as he probably was with everyone else.

"How did you get started, buying companies and so on?"

"A guy in Knoxville needed some help in his welding shop, but he couldn't afford to pay me the going wage. He offered me a working partnership and I accepted. A year and a half later, a larger welding company bought us out. He stayed on to work for them. I took my money and bought into a repair shop where the same thing happened," Brodie explained with marked indifference. "The third time I realized I didn't need a partner and I didn't need to physically work myself. All I had to do was clean out the deadwood, hire people with the skill to do the work, and modernize methods."

"As simple as that," she said with skepticism.

"Yes, it's as simple as that," he agreed.

The waitress stopped at the booth to serve their food. A slice of raw onion rested on a lettuce leaf beside the hamburger on her plate. Jessica glanced at it before adding mustard to her bun.

Brodie noticed her hesitating look. "Go ahead and have the onion. We can buy some breath mints when we leave."

She had never been with any man who was quite so straightforward. The bluntness of his manner flustered her, plus the fact that he seemed capable of reading her every thought. Jessica merely shook her head in refusal of his suggestion. After swallowing a bite of hamburger she sensed her frustration amused him and attempted to divert his attention.

"You mentioned earlier that you wanted to ask me about some of the old crowd. Who, for instance?" she questioned.

The people he named were ones she either

knew or knew about. Jessica suspected he had deliberately chosen people he knew had been friends of either her brother or sister.

When they had finished their hamburgers, Brodie ordered another cup of coffee. Jessica refused the cigarette he offered her and stirred her malt with the straw.

As he bent his head to light his cigarette, she studied the black sheen of his hair. Devil black, she had called it once. It contrasted sharply with the vivid blue of his eyes. His lean, hard features had become encased in a mask that permitted few expressions to flit across its surface.

There were lines crowfooting from the corners of his eyes and grooves slashed into the tan skin on either side of his mouth. It was the compelling face of a self-confident man certain of his ability and his masculinity; two rare characteristics.

His gaze lifted from the cigarette to catch her staring at him. Jessica sipped her malt and tried not to react to the almost physical touch of his look.

"Has the place changed much since you used to come here?" she asked to erase the silence.

"Not much." He glanced disinterestedly around the interior of the restaurant. "It's been repainted and they've moved the jukebox to a different wall. But it's basically the way I remember it."

"It must remind you of a lot of good times," she suggested.

"Yes." Brodie seemed momentarily absent, lost in his thoughts. Then he came back to the present. "It also reminds me of what I never want to go back to being." He took a drink of his coffee and leveled his gaze on her. "We never had much when I was a kid. Our furniture, our car, practically everything we ever owned was secondhand. I was determined that when I grew up, I was going to have the best," he stated.

"Do you have the best now?" Jessica had difficulty meeting his look.

"Not in everything, but I'm working on it." He crushed out his cigarette. "Are you ready to leave?"

"Yes." She pushed her malt aside. It had thinned out to a milky consistency.

Outside in the car, Brodie started the engine. "Would you like to go for a short drive?"

Jessica was tempted to ask their destination but decided against it. The question would have mirrored her distrust, something she preferred to conceal.

"That sounds fine," she agreed instead.

Once they were in the mainstream of traffic, Brodie punched a tape into the stereo tape deck built into the dash. A delicate symphony of strings came from the concealed speakers. He cast her a sideways look.

"I hope you don't object to classical music. I've discovered it's soothing, though I don't pretend to understand the finer techniques of its composition."

"I don't mind. Leave it on."

It had been years since she had listened to a symphonic orchestration, probably not since music class in school, but Jessica found that Brodie was right. The music was quieting and it eliminated the need for conversation — which was a recommendation in itself. She relaxed against the molding backrest of the cushioned passenger seat and listened, watching the blur of passing streetlights.

For a time she kept track of where they were until at some point she lost her sense of direction. It didn't seem really important that she know precisely their whereabouts. There were people and other cars around, homes and businesses. She supposed Brodie was simply taking a tour of the city by night. She closed her eyes for a serene moment, then opened them to study the upholstered ceiling of the car's interior.

The signal blinked in the car to indicate that he was turning onto another street, but Jessica didn't glance out of the window to see where they were going. She was intent on the intricacies of a piano solo coming from the stereo. The car turned again, this time onto a rough surface that bounced her back into an interest in her surroundings.

Brodie was stopping the car in a deserted lot. The nearest building seemed to be some kind of a warehouse. Beyond it, the night's darkness cast eerie shadows on more peculiar-looking objects. Jessica looked back to the empty road. On the other side, a patch of moonlight glittered on water.

Immediately she cast a wary look in Brodie's direction. The darkness shadowed his face, as well, not that she thought his expression would have told her anything. But she didn't need to see to feel his eyes watching her.

"Where are we?" she asked with an attempt at calm. "Is this the place where you used to park with your dates?"

"No, I couldn't afford the gasoline to drive this far." He turned and for a minute his profile was etched by the moonlight. "It would have been a good place, though, private with the moon reflected in the lake."

"Lake?" Was that body of water Lake Chickamauga or the Tennessee River?

"Yes, Lake Chickamauga," Brodie confirmed.

"What are we doing here?" If he wasn't revisiting one of his old haunts, then what was his reason for coming here? Jessica felt her heartbeat accelerate in uncertain alarm.

"There's something 1 want to show you."

With that, he opened his car door and stepped outside. When his door closed, Jessica remained rooted to her seat. She had no idea what he intended to show her and cared even less. Danger signals were ringing in her ears. She hated to admit she was frightened, but she was. After all, he was virtually a stranger.

Her car door was opened and Brodie's hand

was extended to help her out. She stared at it, swallowing hard.

"Come on," he urged.

"Where?"

His throaty chuckle did little to ease her mounting fear.

Chapter Four

"I'm glad you think it's funny," Jessica declared in a burst of irritation.

"Earlier you asked why I'd come back to Chattanooga. I told you only the major reason. I decided to show you the contributing factor. Do you want to see it?" It was a challenge.

All her instincts cried a refusal, but Jessica couldn't show cowardice. Reluctantly she placed her hand in his and stepped from the car.

They had walked several feet toward the darkened building when a voice called out, "The place is closed. You'll have to come back tomorrow during regular business hours."

"You're Art Mason, the security guard, aren't you?" Brodie questioned.

"Yeah?"

"I'm Brodie Hayes. I met you late this afternoon. I want to show the young lady around the place," he stated in a voice that expected his wishes to be granted.

"Sorry, Mr. Hayes," the voice answered immediately. "I didn't recognize you, what with it being so dark and all."

"That's one of the first changes I'm going to make, Mr. Mason." Brodie walked forward, his hand on her waist drawing Jessica along with him. "We're going to have more adequate lighting for the nighttime."

Changes? Had he bought the place? What was it? Jessica stole a glance at his face, but it told her nothing. She could only surmise that her guess was accurate.

A uniformed man in his fifties emerged from the shadow of the building. "That sure will be a welcome change, Mr. Hayes. As it is now, a man's got to have cat's eyes to be able to see anything."

Keys rattled on a metal ring as he bent to unlock the front door. He opened it for them and touched the bill of his cap when Jessica walked past him.

"There's a light switch just inside the door on the left wall, Mr. Hayes," the guard instructed, and shone his flashlight into the building.

Except for that stream of light, it was pitch-black inside the building. The squeezing pressure from Brodie's hand instructed Jessica to stand still, and she waited in the inky blackness until a click illuminated the interior, momentarily blinding her. Then he was by her side again, taking her arm.

"Thank you, Mr. Mason."

"When you leave, just honk your horn and I'll know to lock up," the man said, and closed the door.

A series of offices were in the front of the building. Brodie bypassed them to lead Jessica down the hallway to the rear section. She

looked around for something that would iden-
tify the business.

"Is this your new restoration project?" she
asked.

"Officially it will be at nine o'clock tomorrow
morning when I sign the final purchase agreement," he told her.

"Forgive me for being so ignorant, but what
is this place?"

"Have you heard of Janson Boats?" Brodie
opened a door to a blackened area. "Stay there
a minute until I find the light switch," he added
without giving her a chance to answer his first
question.

Jessica waited. "Janson Boats?" She frowned
while he disappeared into the shadows. "I think
one of our clients was just talking about the
company not too long ago. They manufacture
houseboats, don't they?"

"That's right." A light was switched on to
light up a massive assembly room with large
square-shaped boats in various stages of con-
struction.

"The Janson family started it and sold out
about five years ago," Jessica recalled aloud
what she had heard. "Our client was a friend of
the Jansons. He was saying they were lucky to
get out when they did because the company has
been steadily going downhill."

"Janson had a thriving business when he sold
it. The new owners traded on the reputation
he'd established. They began cutting corners,

60

constructing inferior boats and charging higher prices. They siphoned every dime they could out of the company and into their own pockets. Now that they've skimmed off the cream, they've decided to unload the company and take what they can get."

Brodie was wandering through the assembly room. Jessica followed, picking her way through the debris scattered about the floor, dodging ladders and assorted equipment. The framework skeleton of a boat loomed beside them, and Brodie stopped to examine it.

"Do you know anything about building boats?" She eyed him curiously.

"Not a single thing, except maybe the bow from the stern," he admitted.

Jessica frowned. "Then how will you ever make it a successful concern again?"

Brodie glanced over his shoulder at her and smiled dryly. "That's the ten percent I can buy — money for the man who knows how to build boats."

"But who will you hire?" She wasn't convinced it was as easy as he was implying.

"When I heard the company was in trouble, I nosed around. It seems Janson isn't enjoying his retirement. What's more, he's upset at the way his name has been damaged by the company's practice. I talked to him yesterday and offered him a position as president of Janson Boats, and he accepted."

"Why?"

"Because he wants to work and he wants to see the company become successful again," Brodie explained with commendable patience.

"If that's true, then why didn't he buy the company? Didn't he have the money to buy it?" It didn't make sense to Jessica that a man would go to work for a company that he could own instead.

"Yes, Janson had the money to buy it. But he's getting on in age and liked the idea that he had a nest egg securely tucked away for his old age. He didn't want to risk it in case he couldn't get the company back on its feet again," Brodie explained, as if it were all very logical.

"But you're risking it," she reminded him.

"I don't have anything to lose," he said with a shrug.

"Your money," Jessica pointed out.

"I can afford the loss," he replied with a diffidence that implied just how successful he was.

Jessica fell silent while she absorbed that discovery. Brodie resumed his wandering inspection of the plant area. He was several yards ahead of her before she realized he had moved away. She hurried to catch up with him, unsure whether she could find her way out of this maze alone.

"This will make a very good publicity story for you," she commented.

"What?" He half turned, then agreed, "Yes, the news that Janson is taking over will be good publicity. That fact alone will increase business in the beginning."

"I wasn't thinking of Janson, although it would be good, too. I was referring to you," Jessica explained.

"Me." Brodie paused to measure her with a look. "The boy from the wrong side of town comes home a success, is that how you see it? A Cinderella story in reverse?"

"Something like that," she admitted. "Is that wrong?"

"No, probably not, except that I'm not interested in publicity for myself." The pathway had widened, much of the rubble cleared to one side, enabling them to walk together.

"Why not? It would open a lot of doors for you." Jessica wondered if he was still as eager to be accepted as he once had been.

"Doors that were closed to me before, you mean?" Brodie mocked. "No, thanks. I prefer to open my own doors in my own way."

"That's being stubborn."

"Yes, it is. But I won't be walking into places where I haven't knocked." Brodie pushed back the sleeve of his sweater to check the gold watch on his wrist. "It's getting late and I know you have to work in the morning. Would you like me to take you home now?"

Jessica glanced at her own watch, surprised to see it was much later than she realized. "Yes, please. I just hope you know how to get out of here."

"Through that door." He pointed to his right and Jessica realized they had made a full circle of the assembly room.

She waited in the hallway while he switched off the light, and together they walked to the front entrance. The night watchman wasn't in sight as they closed the door and returned to the car. At the honk of the horn, he appeared and waved his flashlight beam at them before Brodie drove out of the lot onto the street.

The drive back to her apartment complex seemed to take little time, possibly because Jessica spent it thinking about the man behind the wheel and how much she had learned about him in one short evening. There was much more about him that attracted rather than repelled. Yet she still felt a wariness that she couldn't explain. Something cautioned her not to attempt to begin a relationship with him.

They were only a few blocks from her apartment when she felt the need to break the silence. "Do your parents still live here?"

"My father died ten years ago."

Ten years ago, Jessica thought. That was before Brodie achieved his success. She wondered if it bothered him that his father had never lived to see how far he had progressed, but decided the question was too personal.

"I didn't know. I'm sorry," she offered in sympathy.

"There isn't any reason why you should have known about it. You didn't know him," Brodie stated in an unemotional tone.

"No, I didn't know him," Jessica admitted, and fell silent.

"There was something else you wanted to ask me, wasn't there?" He slid a sideways look at her. Jessica nibbled at her lower lip, but didn't answer. "You were wondering about my mother." She caught her breath, stunned that he had guessed so accurately. "I don't know where she is. She and my father were divorced when I was two. An attorney tried to locate her when my father died, but he couldn't find her."

There was absolutely no emotion in his voice, neither bitterness nor remorse that he had never known the woman who had given birth to him. The twinge of pity Jessica felt was wasted. Family had always played an integral part in her life, even now when her relatives lived at a distance. Brodie, obviously, hadn't missed what he had never known.

The car slowed to a stop in front of her apartment building. It took Jessica several seconds to shake out of her reverie. In that time Brodie had got out of the car and walked around to her door.

As she stepped out of the car, a whole new set of thoughts assailed her. The male hand at the small of her back wakened her to the fact that she would soon be bidding Brodie good-night. At the conclusion of every date, with the exception of her first few as a teenager, it was expected that a kiss would be exchanged at the door, but her senses shied vigorously away from the image of his hard mouth pressed against hers.

Her heart was skipping beats when they reached her door. She made a project of searching through her bag for the key. Aware of his eyes watching her, she had the uncanny sensation that Brodie knew exactly what she was thinking, feeling and trying to avoid.

"Thank you for dinner." Her fingers closed around the key at the bottom of her bag.

It struck her then that Brodie might expect her to invite him in for coffee. She had no intention of doing so and wondered how she could delicately avoid it if he suggested it.

"It was my pleasure." Brodie sounded as if he was silently laughing.

Jessica didn't look to see if he was. She removed the key from her bag. But before she could insert it in the lock, Brodie was reaching for it. The touch of his fingers was like scalding water. Jessica surrendered the key to him without resistance and took a step backward to avoid further contact while he unlocked the door.

The bolt clicked open. Jessica trembled when he straightened to face her and tried not to show it. She wondered if it was by design that he was between her and the safety of her apartment.

She held out her hand for the key. "Thank you again. And good luck in your new venture."

She attempted to slide between him and the door, hoping her movement would prompt him to step aside. He didn't. In consequence, she was uncomfortably close to him, and Brodie still hadn't returned the key.

Her gaze focused on the tiny stitches in the sleeve of his sweater while waiting for the key — but not for long. The hand with the key moved toward her. She followed it, expecting the key to be placed in her outstretched hand. Her hand was ignored as his continued in an upward motion that stopped with his forefinger at her chin, the key hidden inside his closed palm.

Forced to meet his gaze, Jessica felt a rushing heat sweep over her skin. One corner of his mouth was a fraction of an inch higher than the other, implying mockery.

"Are you wondering whether I intend to kiss you good-night?" His voice was a slow, lazy drawl, pitched low to lull her into a sense of false security.

How should she respond to that? Laugh it off? Deny that it had even occurred to her that he might kiss her? Or perhaps she should be cool and cutting? She wasn't able to make up her mind which was the best way to handle it. Her indecision gave Brodie command of the situation. Truthfully he had been in charge of the evening from the beginning, and he didn't relinquish the position as it came to an end.

His tracing finger underlined the sensitive

skin from her jaw to her chin and back, a tantalizing caress that sent the pulse in her neck throbbing at an incredible rate. Inside she was a quaking mass of jelly. Outside, there was the faintest quiver.

"I believe —" the finger of the hand with the key slowly worked its way down her neck to the V neckline of her silk blouse, and Jessica was suddenly aware of how deeply it plunged in the front "— you're frightened of me."

She took a breath and lost it as she felt the cool metal of the key being slid inside the lacy cup of her brassiere and against the fiery warmth of her breast. Her stomach was instantly twisted into knots.

"I believe," she began in a voice that was husky from the disturbed state of her nerves, "you're trying to frighten me."

His mouth twitched in a fleeting smile while she silently congratulated herself for having the presence of mind not to reveal how much she was intimidated by his raw virility. It was a small victory, but she cherished it.

"Perhaps I am," Brodie conceded the possible truth in her statement. He was no longer touching her. The lack of actual physical contact didn't lessen the tension that shivered with elemental meanings through her nerves. "But a little fear is good," he added. "It sharpens the senses and sends adrenalin shooting through the veins. It can be very stimulating and exhilarating."

His words defined precisely what Jessica was feeling. She was frightened, but not too frightened to run. The fact made the situation doubly dangerous and placed more power in his hands.

"You can stop wondering, though." His heavily veiled look encompassed every feature of her face. "I'm not going to kiss you goodnight." He turned the knob and pushed the door open, all without taking his eyes from her. Moving aside he added a promise, "Not this time."

Not until Jessica was inside her apartment with the door closed did she realize that he had implied that there would be another time. Yet he hadn't asked her for a date nor even said he would call her. Perhaps because of the pressures of his business, he didn't know when next he would be free.

She listened to the echo of his footsteps in the hallway. The curve of her breast tingled where his hand had made brief contact with it when he had slid the key inside her bra. She took the key and returned it to her bag, but that didn't erase the sensation.

A surge of irritation burned through her as she realized he had taken for granted she would accept a subsequent invitation from him. The only reason she had gone to dinner with him tonight was because she had trapped herself into agreeing. The next time she wouldn't let that happen. Admittedly Brodie Hayes was a fascinating man, but that was all the more reason to stay away from him.

The next few days Jessica lived through in constant anticipation of a telephone call from him, either at work or at home. Yet the weekend came and went without a word from Brodie. At first Jessica blamed the silence on the many loose ends that were probably involved in purchasing the boat-manufacturing company. Then she had assumed that other business interests had taken him out of town.

By the middle of the following week, she was forced to consider that he might not be interested in seeing her again, regardless of what he had implied. That possibility became more logical when Jessica remembered he had admitted taking her to the restaurant where he had wanted to bring her sister. She discovered her ego was bruised. It was one thing to look forward to rejecting him, and quite another to be the one rejected.

While Jessica tried not to admit it, the experience had had an effect on her. She became irritable and defensive. Her patience with others grew short. She pretended that she had forgotten the entire incident, but it was forever nagging at the back of her mind.

There was a knock at the door of her private office. "Yes?" She answered in a voice sharper than she realized.

Ann Morrow, the receptionist, walked in. "A

guy from the printer's dropped this by for you." She handed Jessica a bulky manilla envelope. "He said you'd told him you wanted to go over the proofs as soon as he had them ready."

With a sigh Jessica unfastened the flap. "Do you suppose I'm experienced enough to check copy?" As far as she was concerned, it was something anyone who could read could do, and she found it very boring.

"I wouldn't let it get you down just because Mr. Dane isn't going to let you handle that new account you brought in," Ann insisted.

Jessica raised a dark blond eyebrow and stared at the receptionist. "What new account?" she demanded.

"How many are there, for heaven's sake?" Ann laughed. Before Jessica could reply that she knew of none, she was interrupted by the ring of the telephone in the reception room. "Ooops, I'd better get that."

Jessica watched her leave, for a minute overcome by curiosity. Then she shrugged. Ann must have got her information confused. She knew nothing about a new client. It must have been someone else in the office who had solicited the new account. In any event, her uncle hadn't mentioned anything about it to her yet, but she generally heard about new accounts in a roundabout way.

She took the proof copies out of the envelope and began checking them. The first glaring error fairly leaped off the page at her as she noted that the wrong size of type had been used. Farther down the same page the wrong style of type had been set.

The instructions had been very explicit and it angered Jessica that they had been so blatantly ignored. She raced through the rest of it and found three more mistakes, minor ones. As far as she was concerned, they were marks of shoddy workmanship.

Bundling the corrected copy back into its envelope, she called the printing company, told them what she thought of the quality of their work, and instructed them to have someone return immediately for the proofs. Much of her anger had been vented in the phone call, but a trace of it was still shimmering in the green of her eyes when she entered the outer office.

"A man from the printing company is to be here within the hour to pick this up," she informed Ann as she tossed the envelope on her desk.

"At lunchtime? But I'll be gone," Ann protested.

Jessica glanced at her watch. It was eleven-thirty. "I didn't realize what time it was," she apologized with irritation at her oversight. "Just leave it on your desk, then."

As she turned, the door to her uncle's office opened and Brodie Hayes walked out. His blue eyes lighted on her immediately and a half smile curved his mouth while she tried to get her breath back. Again he was dressed in a dark suit and tie that emphasized the darkness of his looks and gave the impression of a prosperous businessman.

It was a full second before Jessica became aware of the stranger who was with him as well as her uncle. Ann's comment about a new client clicked in her mind. Had she meant Brodie?

"Hello, Jessica," Brodie greeted her, but didn't give her an opportunity to answer. "I don't believe you've met Mr. Janson."

Jessica managed a smile as she stepped forward. Janson was the man who had agreed to take over the presidency of the company he had once owned. He was a sparely built man with bushy eyebrows and a mass of iron gray hair. The harshness of his features was softened when he smiled, as he was doing now. Jessica had the feeling he was a very honest, trustworthy man.

"It's indeed a pleasure to meet you, Miss Thorne." The man shook her hand and cast a glance sideways at Brodie. "I can certainly see why Mr. Hayes found you so persuasive."

"Persuasive?" She was confused, and a glance at Brodie only added to it.

"There's no need to be modest, Jessica." The unsettling blue eyes were fixed on her. "Mr. Janson has already added his endorsement to your suggestions."

"My suggestions?" She was beginning to feel like an echo.

"Yes, and they were very good, too," her uncle inserted. "The campaign you outlined to Mr. Hayes will be just the thing to rebuild the reputation of the company. Janson back at the helm," Ralph Dane said as if quoting a line from an advertisement.

Nothing was making any sense to her. She didn't know what they were talking about. She had made no suggestions for a campaign nor even suggested that Brodie should use this firm. But before she could correct the impression, Brodie was speaking.

"You can handle everything from here, Cal," he told Janson, and turned to her uncle. "It was a pleasure meeting you, Mr. Dane. While you two have lunch, I hope you don't mind if I spirit your niece away for an early lunch of our own."

"I certainly don't," her uncle smiled broadly.

"But —" Jessica began.

"Where's your coat?" Brodie interrupted.

"In my office." There was more she would have said, but his hand was already on her elbow directing her to her office.

Chapter Five

Brodie ushered Jessica into her office and closed the door. She turned to face him, his bland expression telling her absolutely nothing.

"Would you mind explaining to me what's going on?" Her hands were on her hips in challenge.

"Over lunch. Where's your coat?" he repeated his earlier question, then noticed the coat hanging on a wall hook.

Jessica was much too confused to object when he helped her into it and handed her shoulder bag to her. He was guiding her to the outer office before Jessica realized how readily she was falling in with his plans. She pulled her arm free of his hold.

"What are you doing?" she demanded.

"I'm taking you to lunch," he responded.

"I never said I'd go with you."

Brodie tipped his head to an inquiring angle. "Will you?"

"I have no intention of going anywhere with you." Jessica set her handbag on the chair and started to slip out of her coat.

"The same way you had no intention of providing me with your address." His hands were on her shoulders, as if to help her off with the coat.

Something in his voice made her pause. "What are you talking about?" She feigned ignorance.

"I'm talking about the last time you accepted my invitation to dinner, knowing that I didn't know where you lived and doubting that I would find out." His hands remained on her shoulders, his closeness a tangible thing.

Jessica's back was to him, but the warmth of his hands seemed to burn through the coat to her skin. "You knew!" The murmur was halfway between an accusation and an admission.

"Yes, I knew."

"Why did you bother to find out where I lived when you guessed what I did?" She lifted her head to a proudly defensive angle, refusing to feel guilty for her act.

"I invited you to dinner. You accepted. I always do what I say I'm going to do and I expect the reverse to be true with others, when necessary, by helping them fulfill their word." With one hand, Brodie turned her around and slipped his other hand inside her coat to rest on the curve of her waist.

The floor seemed to rock beneath her feet. Tipping her head back to look at his malely defined face, Jessica was reminded again that Brodie got what he wanted, one way or another. Resistance seemed futile.

"Shall we have lunch?" he asked, as if suggesting it for the first time.

All she had to do was refuse. Since he had revealed his knowledge of her previous deception, she felt trapped. She was honor bound to go with him. Reluctantly she nodded agreement.

Brodie stepped away and held the door to the outer office open for her. Flipping her blond hair free of the coat collar, Jessica swept past him. She paused at the receptionist's desk, trying to ignore the imposing man accompanying her.

"If anyone calls, I've gone to lunch. Be sure to leave that envelope for the printer," she instructed. "I'll be back around one o'clock."

"Maybe," Brodie inserted.

Before Jessica could contradict him, he was ushering her outside. The last thing that registered was the faintly envious gleam in the receptionist's eyes. Silently she acknowledged that Brodie was capable of turning heads. He had caught her attention when they had both been waiting at the crosswalk. Because he had seemed familiar, she had continued to stare at him that time, but it had definitely been his commanding male presence that had first drawn her eye. So it really wasn't so surprising that Ann had been drawn by it, too.

"I thought we'd have lunch at the railway station," Brodie said as he helped Jessica into his car parked at the curb. "Is that all right?"

"Fine," she agreed with an indifferent air that said she didn't care where they lunched.

There was no further attempt at conversation

as Brodie negotiated the luxury car through the city traffic and onto the street where the renovated railroad station of the Chattanooga Choo-Choo was located.

"I suppose you've eaten here many times before," Brodie commented after they had parked the car in the lot and entered the station remodeled to house assorted shops and restaurants.

"Not recently," she replied coolly.

"I hope you don't mind coming here." He led her to the high-ceilinged restaurant. "I've never been here before — I couldn't afford it."

It was an offhand statement, without apology, that instantly reminded Jessica of his background. He handled his new status with the ease of one who had been accustomed to having everything he wanted all his life. She was forced to remember that it hadn't always been so. Brodie had fought his way to the top and shouldn't be underestimated.

The tables in the restaurant were nearly all full, mostly with tourists. Within minutes, Brodie had persuaded the hostess to find them a table at the window with a view of the gardens. The sun glared through the skylight. Jessica had just opened her menu when the waiter appeared.

"Two glasses of white wine, please. We'll order later." Brodie set his menu aside.

"I do have to be back by one," Jessica stated.

"It won't hurt if you're late," he insisted with

infuriating complacency.

She gritted her teeth for an instant. "I know you believe that because my employer is also my uncle, I can come and go as I please, but that doesn't happen to be true. I have work to do, work that I'm paid to do."

"Your uncle is not going to object if you take a longer lunch today." He paused as the waiter brought their wine. "Especially since you're lunching with me. After all, I'm a new client and my account with your uncle's firm promises to be very large."

"That's another thing," Jessica seized on that. "What was all that nonsense about me persuading you to bring the Janson account to us? I had nothing to do with it."

"Don't be naïve, Jessica." His mouth curved above the rim of the wine glass. "You had everything to do with it. You're the reason, the only reason, I ordered Janson to have Dane handle the advertising."

Jessica swallowed, his bluntness throwing her again. "Why me?" God, she didn't know why she asked that question. She'd give anything to have it back.

"Because you have blond hair and green eyes. Because you're a woman I want to get to know . . . very well." The slight hesitation was designed to underline the last two words. Their message was unmistakable. Jessica felt the blood rush hotly through her veins. His observant blue eyes noted her reaction. "Hasn't a man ever made a pass at you before?" Brodie mocked cruelly.

"Of course." She tried to shrug away his question with a worldliness she didn't feel at the moment. Self-consciously, she fingered the stem of her wine glass.

"And?" he prompted.

"And what?" Jessica tried to appear nonchalant.

"And what would you do if I made a pass at you?"

A table separated them. Yet the way he was looking at her made her feel he was making love to her in his mind. She could almost feel the caress of his hands causing the curling sensation in the pit of her stomach, and it awakened a primitive hunger that had nothing to do with food.

"I guess you'll have to wait and find out." She clung to her air of bravado, despite the fact that she was rawly vulnerable.

"I'll look forward to it. But don't worry." He smiled lazily. "I'm not going to rush you."

"Am I supposed to be grateful that you warned me?" she retorted.

"Do you consider it a warning?" An eyebrow quirked thoughtfully. "I thought it was a promise."

"We'd better order." Jessica picked up her menu, finding she was no match for him in this battle of innuendoes.

"You've eaten here before." Brodie didn't object to her suggestion. "What would you recommend?"

"Since I'm not familiar with your tastes, I can't help you." She refused to look up from the menu, her pulse was running away with her.

"But you know my tastes. I want only the best. Nothing less will do." His disconcerting blue gaze was leveled at her, and she sensed that he wasn't referring to food.

"My definition of that might differ from yours. You'll have to choose for yourself," she insisted. "I'm going to have the chef's salad."

Brodie motioned the waiter to their table, gave him Jessica's order and his own for a rare steak. As raw as she felt, she thought his choice was somehow fitting. It was even more nerve-racking to know that he was aware of what he was doing to her.

"Don't you care for the wine?" Brodie asked.

Jessica had yet to take a sip of it. "I generally don't care to have anything to drink during the day."

"But this is a special occasion."

"Why?"

"Because we're here together, you and I." He took a drink from his glass and set it down. "I was beginning to think there would always be an appointment, a telephone call to make, something to prevent me from seeing you again."

"Really?" she murmured.

"Do you mean you didn't expect to hear

from me before today?" His question was faintly taunting.

"I didn't think about you at all," Jessica lied.

"Did you really believe I wouldn't be back to claim a good-night kiss?" His gaze slid to her lips and Jessica had to fight an impulse to moisten them.

"Isn't there something else we can discuss?" she demanded in irritation while her fingers nervously traced a circle around the rim of her wine glass.

"Something of lesser importance such as the weather?" Brodie asked.

"I don't care what it is. The weather or the cost of a loaf of bread, it makes no difference," Jessica breathed out impatiently.

"Then stop playing with the wine glass like that."

Her hand jerked from the glass as if it had suddenly caught fire. She folded her hands in her lap and struggled to regain her momentary loss of poise. Fortunately, their waiter chose that moment to arrive with their meal, which smoothed over Jessica's sensation of inadequacy.

Yet it was a relief when each had finished and Brodie signaled the waiter for their check. She, who had thought herself so experienced, had discovered that she didn't know how to handle this man. Brodie was in control, directing events, conversations and feelings.

As they left the restaurant, Jessica started toward the exit to the parking lot, but the pressure of Brodie's hand forestalled her.

"You still have plenty of time to get back to the office. Why don't we wander through the shops?" he suggested smoothly.

She hesitated. The trouble was he was right. It was well before one o'clock yet. Still she attempted to wiggle out of it.

"They just have the usual assortment of things," she said, shrugging.

He raised an eyebrow. "A woman who doesn't care to browse? That's rare."

He made it sound like a compliment. Out of sheer perversity, Jessica turned into the entrance of the first shop, determined to look at every single item. If he became bored, that was just his tough luck.

After a short time, it wasn't difficult to pretend an interest in the various items. Jessica was aware of Brodie strolling along behind her, pausing when she stopped to inspect something that had caught her eye, but she did a credible job of ignoring him.

A pair of candlestick holders carved out of oak particularly attracted her attention. The workmanship in the set was flawless.

"They're beautiful, aren't they?" she admired them aloud, holding one to more closely examine the intricate carving on the base.

"Yes, they are," Brodie agreed.

A few minutes later Jessica moved on to several shelves of pottery. Within seconds, she sensed there was something wrong. She turned around and found she was alone; Brodie was no longer with her. She glanced around the shop and saw him walking away from the cash register, carrying a package. A furrow of puzzled curiosity drew her brows together as he approached her.

"For you." Brodie offered her the package and added the explanation, "The candlestick holders you liked."

Her gaze jumped from the package to his chiseled features. "But I didn't mean that I wanted you to buy them for me."

"I know you didn't." He forced the package into her hand. "But I wanted you to have them."

Jessica unfastened the clasp of her bag and, with one hand, tried to find her wallet. "I'll pay for them."

His hand curved along the side of her neck, his thumb forcing her chin up. "Didn't your parents teach you how to accept a present graciously?" he chided. "You smile very prettily and say 'thank you.'"

He touched her without a trace of self-consciousness. It was done with such ease, so naturally, as if he was long accustomed to treating her so familiarly. The sensations his touch created were not familiar to Jessica.

"My parents did teach me not to take candy from strangers," she offered in defense, fighting the breathlessness that changed her voice.

His intensely blue gaze commanded that she

look at him. "But we won't be strangers for long, Jessica."

It became easier to surrender than struggle against a superior force. "Thank you. They're beautiful," she accepted the gift with stiff gratitude.

"Now the smile," Brodie prodded. Only when she gave it to him did he take his hand away from the slender curve in her throat. "Shall we go look at the model-train display?"

"Yes," Jessica agreed readily with his suggestion.

Although the pressure of his hand had been in no way threatening, the sensation of danger faded when it was taken away. Her heart continued to beat at an uneven tempo, but she didn't feel quite as weak as she had a minute before.

Leaving the gift shop, they walked outside onto the platform of the old train depot to the store with the model-train display. The display, which occupied almost an entire room, was a scale model of Chattanooga, complete with trains, tracks, tunnels, bridges and detailed structures to scale. Miniature trees forested a replica of Lookout Mountain. Houses had clotheslines and there were women hanging clothes.

As the model trains, passenger cars and locomotives, raced around the tracks, barely missing each other at switching stations and crossings, there was always some new facet to see. It captured the imagination of young and old alike.

"It's fascinating, isn't it?" Jessica watched the precise timing that miraculously avoided any crashes of locomotives. "Justin had a model train set up in his room. Nothing as large as this, of course. His was built on a wooden table. Whenever he had it running, he used to let me come in and watch. He always insisted I was too young to operate it."

"When you were old enough, I imagine you became more interested in boys, pop stars, and girl talk than model trains," Brodie concluded.

"Something like that," she admitted.

A little boy's voice echoed clearly through the room. "Can I have that, daddy?" His arm swept out to indicate the entire display.

"We don't have a room large enough for it," the man holding him answered. "But maybe Santa can bring you *one* train for Christmas. Is that all right?"

"Will it make smoke like that one?" the boy pointed.

"Yes, it will make smoke," the father agreed.

"That's okay, then. Santa can bring me that." The boy accepted the compromise offer.

A smile tugged at the corners of Jessica's mouth. "I'll bet every child that sees this wants a train for Christmas." She glanced up at Brodie through the sweep of her lashes, idly curious. "Did Santa ever bring you a train for Christmas, one that blows smoke?"

"No, I never did get a train." He shook his head briefly, his black hair gleaming. "But there were a lot of Christmases that Santa didn't make it to our house. I'm not sure whether it was because we were too poor or because I was a bad boy."

Rather than comment on his background, Jessica chose a facetious remark. "Santa always knows who's been good or bad."

"He certainly knows that I didn't make my father's life any easier." His hands were braced on the railing that cordoned off the public from the display. "My father used to work for the railroad."

"He did?" Jessica was glad he had changed the subject. The memory of her brother saying that Brodie was no good was still very clear in her mind.

"Yes. He was hurt in a derailment when I was about five and ended up partially disabled. He never was able to get enough part-time work to combine with his pension to give us enough to live on, and he was too damned proud to go on welfare, so we went without a lot of things."

"What was your father like?" She tried to visualize an older version of Brodie, but had difficulty picturing a disabled man when Brodie was so vital and robust.

"Stubborn, proud. The one thing he couldn't tolerate was failure. In the end, he was a broken man." His gaze narrowed on the miniature tracks of the display. "He couldn't work at the job he loved — the railroad. His wife had run out on him. His son brought him pain instead of hope."

"I'm sorry, Brodie." This time Jessica wasn't offering empty words. "He would have been proud of you today."

"Yes." Brodie straightened from the rail, his action indicating that he was ready to leave the model-train display. "But it didn't work out that way."

She marveled that he could accept it so calmly, but he'd had more time to adjust to it. He'd had to put the remorse behind him and carry on with his life, while she was just tasting the bitter pangs of disappointment on his behalf for the first time.

They wandered outside again, onto the platform. The locomotive of the famed Chattanooga Choo-Choo waited on Track 29 of the 1905 Terminal Station. A collection of dining cars and sleeping-parlor cars occupied more mock tracks within the center.

"Have you ever eaten in one of the dining cars?" Brodie asked when Jessica slowed her steps for a closer look at one.

"No." She smiled wryly. "Isn't that typical? You never take advantage of attractions in your own hometown."

"True," he agreed.

"My intentions have been good, but I've never been able to get reservations on the night

I wanted to go." She shrugged at the thwarted opportunities.

"We'll both have to correct this oversight, since I've never dined there, either. I'll make reservations to dine here some evening when I'm in town."

He was taking her acceptance for granted, something Jessica couldn't allow. "As long as I happen to be free the same evening."

"Of course," he said with a look that expressed confidence that she would be available.

They continued to stroll along the platform. As they approached a group of tourists occupying much of the platform, Brodie's hand moved to a spot between Jessica's shoulders to guide her through the throng. The vaguely possessive touch sent quivers down her spine, especially when his hand slid downward to the back of her waist.

"I understand the parlor cars are actually rented out. Couples can spend the night in them," Brodie commented.

"That's true. I've seen pictures of the interior. They're beautiful — Victorian furniture, brass beds." Jessica told him.

"When I make our dinner reservations, maybe I should reserve us a sleeping car." His sideways glance inspected her face.

Jessica felt it grow warm. "No, thank you."

"Does the thought of making love embarrass you?" Again his candor unnerved her. "Or isn't it proper for women of breeding to discuss such things?"

She didn't want to answer either question. She was on treacherous footing. The sooner she reached solid ground, the better off she would be.

"It must be time for me to get back to the office," she offered desperately.

Brodie glanced at his watch and mocked, "So it is. Always the conscientious employee, aren't you?"

"I earn my salary." She refused to sound righteous.

They turned and started back for the parking lot. "And do you work Saturdays, as well?"

"No, the office is closed on Saturdays." Her steps quickened.

"That doesn't mean you don't work. Officially, the office may be closed, but there still may be work to do," he reasoned.

"So far I haven't had to work on Saturday," was the only answer Jessica could give.

"What do you do, then? Play tennis? Golf? Swim?"

"It depends."

"What will you be doing this Saturday?" Brodie asked.

"I don't have anything special planned." Immediately Jessica realized she had fallen into another one of his traps.

"In that case, we can plan something together," he decided.

"If you have in mind that sleeping car . . ." she began with rising indignation.

"Actually what I had in mind is a tour of some of Chattanooga's attractions. A day spent sight-seeing. Is that innocent enough for you?" A wicked light glinted in his eyes.

"I suppose so. . . ." Again it was an invitation that left her without grounds to refuse. Part of her didn't want to refuse, either.

"Good. I'll pick you up at your apartment at ten Saturday morning." It was all settled.

Chapter Six

Saturday morning was flooded with sunshine. There wasn't a cloud in the crystal-blue sky as it formed a contrasting backdrop to the spring green of the land. The white flowers of the dogwood blossomed in the hills. The air was filled with mating calls from the trilling song of birds to the chattering cries of squirrels.

Jessica stood on the narrow balcony of her apartment to watch and listen. A loose-fitting silk blouse of olive green, its color a shade darker than her eyes, was belted at the waist over a pair of white Levis. A long, chunky chain of gold hung around her neck.

It was a warm, coatless day, certainly not the kind of day one wanted to spend indoors. But of course she wasn't. Jessica glanced at the gold watch on her wrist; one minute before ten. As if on cue, the doorbell rang.

Her heart gave a sudden leap of excitement and she paused until it had resumed its normal rate. It was essential to keep both feet on the ground today. It would never do to be carried away by spring fever, a malady she was susceptible to.

The doorbell rang a second time as she turned the knob and opened the door wide. Her heart became lodged in her throat at the sight of Brodie, despite her effort to keep it firmly in its place. He seemed so potently male standing there.

A white shirt stretched across his wide shoulders to taper to his waist, the long sleeves rolled halfway up his forearms, the top three buttons unfastened. A pair of brushed denims hugged his hips and emphasized the long length of his legs. But it was the impression of so much tanned, hard flesh that was causing the most havoc with her senses.

"Hello." His greeting had a velvet quality to it. "This is for you — a rose for a Thorne, if you'll forgive an overworked sentiment."

Until Brodie offered it to her, Jessica hadn't noticed the single red rose in his hand. Her fingers curled around the stem to take it from him, the carnelian red petals in full bloom.

"It's beautiful," she murmured inadequately. "Thank you."

"Are you ready?"

"Yes. Just give me a moment to put this in a vase."

She hurried into the kitchen, took a bud vase from the cupboard, and partially filled it with water. Standing the rose stem in the vase, she carried it into the living room and set it next to the mantel clock where the polished grains of the wood would show off the rich red of the flower.

Brodie watched it all from inside the doorway, commenting when Jessica joined him,

"If I'd known you were going to go to all that trouble, I would have brought you a bouquet."

"It was no trouble."

In the hallway, Brodie waited while she locked the door. "Have you had breakfast?"

"Toast and coffee." Generally she ate a hearty breakfast, but she didn't want to dwell on why she hadn't been hungry this morning.

"Good. I didn't have time to eat, either. Instead of lunch, let's have a late breakfast," he suggested.

"Very well," she agreed.

Considering her lack of appetite earlier, Jessica was surprised to discover she was almost ravenous when the waitress set a plate of bacon, eggs, grits and biscuits in front of her. Brodie's meal was similarly huge. Neither had difficulty cleaning the plates.

"Have you had enough or would you like something more?" he asked.

"More than enough," she declared with a decisive nod. "I'm going to need to exercise to work it off."

"That can be arranged." There was a smile in his voice as he lifted the coffee cup to his mouth. Draining all but the dregs, he set the cup down. "Shall we go?"

At her nod of agreement, he paid for the breakfast and they left. Outside in the car, he started the engine but didn't put it in gear, turning an inquiring look at her.

"Where would you like to start our tour?"

Jessica had no preference. "You're the driver — you choose."

A lazy look of wickedness stole over his face. "Aren't you concerned that I'll choose the sleeping car at the Train Station in order to provide you with that exercise you said you needed?"

This time his suggestive comment did not completely shatter her poise. "That isn't the kind of exercise I had in mind," she answered with a commendable show of calm.

"What did you have in mind? Something more tame and less stimulating, like walking?" Brodie mocked.

He directed his gaze at her lips to watch them form the words of her answer. The action tested the strength of her composure. It held.

"Yes, like walking."

"In that case, we'll start our tour at the top by beginning at Lookout Mountain." Brodie shifted the car into gear and finally looked away from her.

The mountain towered at the edge of the city like a sentinel. Access to the top was by a road that twisted and curved its way up the slope. As they neared the entrance to Rock City, one of the more popular tourist attractions on top of Lookout Mountain, Brodie glanced at Jessica.

"I never thought about it, but it probably would have been quicker to take the Incline," he said.

"I prefer driving to the top. That railway is

95

too steep for me." The one and only time Jessica had ridden it, it had seemed to go straight up the mountain, so steep was the incline.

"Do heights bother you?" Brodie eyed her curiously.

"Yes." She didn't lie about the phobia she had for high places.

Although he didn't comment, she had the sensation that Brodie stored the information away. He parked the car in the lot opposite Rock City Gardens and they walked across the street to the entrance, a building that didn't attempt to compete with the natural splendor that lay beyond it.

A trail wound its way through ageless rock formations, majestic and massive. Trees grew where it seemed impossible that they could root. There was a springtime explosion of flowers that filled the air with their delicate scents. The myriad sights, sounds and smells demanded a leisurely pace.

Jessica lingered at the balancing rock to study its seeming defiance of gravity. "It's been so long since I was here that I'd forgotten how unique this place is." She glanced at Brodie, remembering his previous comments about the deprivation of his childhood. "Have you ever been here before?"

"My father brought me here a couple of times when I was small. The last time I was here, though, I was thrown out." His mouth

96

quirked at the memory.

"Why? What did you do?"

"I didn't have enough money to get in, so I snuck in without paying. Unfortunately — or fortunately, depending on your point of view, I was caught."

As they continued along the trail past the balancing rock, his hand seemed to automatically seek hers. The grip of his hand was strong and firm. Jessica doubted that she could have pulled her hand free of it — not that she wanted to. She discovered that she liked this sensation of being linked to him. She was content to enjoy the feeling rather than question the wisdom of it.

Without referring to her fear of heights, Brodie guided her away from the swinging bridge that spanned a chasm in the park and chose the more solid alternative of the stone bridge instead.

At Lovers' Leap, Jessica gravitated unconsciously toward the Eagles' Nest, a man-made aperture that jutted out from the rock face of the mountain. The view was spectacular from the observation point. The air was crystal clear except for a thin band of haze on the distant Great Smoky Mountains. The vivid green of the land contrasted with the sharp blue of the sky, a combination of colors only nature could make.

At the foot of the mountain was Chattanooga. Close to that was the Civil War battlefield of Chickamauga where the South had won its last major victory. But it was the far beyond, the distant horizons, that stunned the imagination. Here was a view of seven states. Directly south was the rolling landscape of Georgia and Alabama. Working north came South Carolina, North Carolina, Virginia, and finally Tennessee and Kentucky.

So wrapped up was she in the sprawling vistas, Jessica wasn't aware of how close she was to the edge until she accidentally looked down. A cold chill ran through her bones, freezing her heartbeat for a terrifying second.

An arm circled her shoulders and turned her away from the edge. Her heart started beating again and she darted a grateful look at Brodie. His smile was gentle but fleeting. Once they were away from the edge and back on the trail through the park, he took his arm from her shoulders, but made no attempt to hold her hand.

"That was quite a view, wasn't it?" he offered in idle conversation.

"In every direction except down." Her attempt at laughter wavered from her throat.

"I wondered how long it would take before you realized where you were standing." There wasn't a trace of sympathy in his voice, only faint amusement.

Jessica felt suddenly defensive. "Everyone has a weakness. What's yours?"

Brodie stopped and looked her over, his direct gaze lingering on her honey-colored hair before meeting her eyes. "Women with blond hair and green eyes."

Over his shoulder there was the sparkling silver ribbon of a waterfall, but Jessica didn't notice it nor the fellow sightseers scattered along the trail. She was aware of nothing but the man in front of her and the sudden tightness that had gripped her throat.

"Is that right?" She tried to make it a breezy retort, but it came out breathless.

"Yes." Relentlessly he held her gaze. "I read somewhere that a gentleman shouldn't kiss a lady until the third date. Counting lunch, this is the third time we've been out together, Green Eyes. I don't remember if it said when a gentleman is entitled to claim his kiss, but. . . ." His hand molded itself to the curve of her neck, his long fingers sliding into the silky length of her hair at the back of her neck. His other hand cupped the side of her face, lifting her chin with his thumb. "I'm not going to wait any longer."

His mouth made a slow, unhurried descent to her lips. There was ample time to protest, but Jessica didn't utter a sound. The curiosity to discover his kiss was overpowering. As the distance lessened, her eyes slowly closed.

Then his mouth was warmly covering hers, its touch firm and experienced. At its persuasive movement on her lips, the tension of anticipation eased and Jessica responded to the kiss.

Her hands spread over his rib cage for support, feeling his hard flesh through the thin material of his shirt. The arching of her spine enabled the rest of her body to lean closer to his male length. Resistance melted as a slow burning fire spread through her veins.

The pressure of the kiss was ended, but he didn't move his mouth from her lips. "I've been wanting to do that for a long time," he murmured against their softness.

Jessica found herself wishing that he hadn't waited so long. In the next second, that thought was banished under the driving possession of his mouth. The pressure at the back of her neck lifted her on tiptoes. She felt drawn to the edge of a precipice, the ground quaking beneath her feet, creating shudders within her.

"Don't look down. Just hold onto me," Brodie muttered thickly as if he knew exactly what she was feeling.

In blind obedience, her hands curved around to his muscled back, fingers curling into the material of his shirt stretched taut by the flexing muscles. The biting hold of his hands on her head and neck caused pain, but Jessica didn't object to it. An inner voice told her that if Brodie ever let her go, she would never recover from the fall.

Gradually she became aware that he was letting her down slowly. The ground beneath her feet became solid. She was no longer balanced on the edge of her toes, but was standing squarely. In another few seconds the warmth of his mouth was no longer on hers. Before his hands left her face, they smoothed her hair. Reluctantly she opened her eyes, hoping she didn't look as dazed as she felt.

Brodie was glancing around them, his attention only returning to her face when he sensed her eyes were on him. A smoldering light was visible through the banked blue fire of his gaze.

"We have an audience." His comment implied that he would not have stopped otherwise.

Jessica felt no embarrassment at the announcement. "Perhaps it's as well we do," she murmured.

Brodie didn't respond to that. By mutual consent, they continued along the trail through the rock garden to its end. From there, their tour included Ruby Falls, the Chickamauga battlefield, and very late in the afternoon, a stop for sandwiches.

Not once did either of them allude to the kiss by the waterfall. Yet Jessica was aware that what had begun as a reluctant attraction to a charismatic man had become something physical. The slightest touch of him vividly recalled the more intimate contact. There was a part of her that didn't regret the change.

When Brodie stopped the car in front of the apartment building, she had the feeling that the afternoon had ended too soon. As he took the key from the ignition, his comment seemed to echo her thought.

"I wish I'd had that second cup of coffee the waitress offered back at the restaurant." He stepped out of the car and walked around to her side.

"If you like, I can make some coffee," Jessica offered.

There was a mocking twinkle in his eye that gave him a roguish look as he closed the door after she had climbed out. "I thought you'd never ask!"

Inside her apartment, she motioned toward the living room. "Make yourself comfortable while I fix the coffee."

She continued on to the kitchen, fighting a sudden attack of nerves. After she had rinsed out the glass pot, she turned to find Brodie had followed her into the kitchen.

"I never have figured out how I'm supposed to make myself comfortable sitting alone in a strange room," he explained his presence in the kitchen.

"I've felt the same way myself," Jessica laughed. "I always end up sitting on the edge of the chair waiting for the other person to come back. It's awkward."

However many times she had felt that way, she had never once admitted it to the host or hostess. Yet Brodie had, with casual frankness.

Measuring the fresh coffee grounds into the filter, she slipped it into its place in the coffee maker. Brodie watched, his arms crossed in front of him, a hip leaned against the kitchen counter. Jessica filled a plastic container with the proper amount of water and poured it into the coffee maker. She flipped the Brew switch to the On position.

"It won't be long," she promised him.

Brodie was standing in front of the cupboard where the plastic water container belonged. As she approached, Jessica had the sensation that all of him was watching her — not just his eyes, but his other senses were observing her, as well. She found herself wishing that she had had time to freshen her lipstick, brush her hair to a silken texture, dab on some perfume behind her ears.

As she reached past him to put the container in the cupboard Brodie straightened to avoid the door. "It doesn't matter about the coffee."

Jessica stared at him. "Why didn't you say so before I made it?"

"We both know it was just an excuse. An excuse so you could invite me in and an excuse for me to accept." Brodie sliced through any attempt at pretense. "You'll pour me a cup and I'll drink it." He reached out to span her waist with his hands and pull her closer to him. "But this is why we're here."

She flattened her hands against his chest in a weak attempt at protest even as she lifted her head to accept his kiss. It was hard and demanding, parting her lips to deepen the passion that sprang between them like a living flame. Her hands slid around his neck, her fingers seeking the sensual thickness of his black hair.

His own were molding her back and hips, crushing her softer flesh to the unyielding contours of his body. The heady scent of his masculine cologne, the intimate taste of his mouth, the thudding of his heart against hers — they all combined to dominate her senses. Jessica realized that she was losing control, not just of her flesh, but of her will, too.

It was much too soon. She couldn't surrender to someone she barely knew. She twisted away from the possession of his kiss only to quiver with desire as Brodie nibbled at the sensitive cord of her neck. Her muscles tensed an instant before she pushed herself out of his embrace, but he didn't pursue when she took a shaky step away.

Jessica avoided his gaze. "I just remembered I have some cake in the refrigerator." She realized that she was probably babbling like an idiot, but she couldn't endure the sudden silence. She started toward the refrigerator. "It's bought cake, but it's really very good. Would you like a piece with your coffee?"

When she would have opened the door to get the cake, Brodie's hand was there to close it and turn her around. Jessica took a step backward, bumping into the refrigerator, the smooth finish cool against her shoulders.

Brodie leaned a hand on the refrigerator near her head.

"No, I would not like any cake." He slowly enunciated each word.

Without touching any other part of her, he bent his head to kiss her. He displayed a hunger for her lips, tasting them, eating them, and rearousing her appetite for his. Their mouths strained for each other, but their bodies made no other contact.

Finally Brodie disentangled his mouth from hers and straightened while Jessica leaned weakly against the refrigerator, her pulse thudding in her ears. He reached out to trace her features with his fingers, his thumb outlining the curve of her mouth. His other hand drew a line from the point of her chin to the hollow of her throat. Then both slid to her shoulders, erotically kneading her flesh, and Jessica shuddered at the wave of intense longing that rushed through her.

"Don't tremble," Brodie ordered softly. The sound of his voice proved almost as provocative as the upheaval his hands were causing. "I'm not going to make love to you, Jessica. I don't have time to do it properly."

"You don't?" Was she relieved or disappointed? She was so incapable of coherent thought that she didn't know.

"No, I don't have time. I have to leave." His fingers suddenly dug into her flesh to pull her away from the refrigerator. He kissed her hard and swiftly, then let her go. "The coffee is done. Pour me a cup."

He walked to the dinette table and sat in one of the chairs, while Jessica tried to gather her scattered senses. It seemed unjust that he would destroy her this way, then announce that he had to leave. Irritation helped to steady her hand as she filled two mugs with coffee.

"Are you sure you have time to drink this?" An acid ring crept into her question.

Amusement glittered as he detected the tone. "I wouldn't have asked you to pour if I thought I didn't."

"I wouldn't want to make you late for an appointment." Jessica set one mug on the table in front of him.

His hand closed around her wrist to take the other coffee cup from her hand and set it on the table beside his. Before she could guess his intention, Brodie was turning her around to sit her on his lap.

"You've already made me late." He took a punishing nibble on her earlobe. One large hand held both of hers prisoner in her lap. Jessica was disturbingly aware of the muscular solidness of his thighs beneath her. "My plane is waiting at the airport."

She realized that when he said he was leaving, he had meant leaving town. "Where are you going?"

"Nashville." He adjusted the collar of her blouse, then let the tip of his finger explore the shadowy cleft. "I have to be there by seven-thirty. I was supposed to be there at noon today, but I was able to postpone the meeting until to-night, just so I could spend today with you."

"I. . . ." Jessica didn't know what to say. "I didn't know."

"Maybe now you'll understand just how de-termined I am to have you." Brodie regarded her steadily, his blue eyes unwavering.

She wasn't sure how he meant that, but at the moment it didn't seem important. "When will you be coming back?"

"One day next week." His hand moved down to rub her thigh. "I don't know which one — I'll have to call you."

He was taking it for granted that she wanted to hear from him again. Jessica didn't mind, be-cause it was suddenly and unexpectedly vital that she did.

"My telephone number isn't listed."

"I already have the number," Brodie said.

"How did you get it?" She frowned.

"When I was here the other night, I copied it off the telephone in the living room." He flashed her a mocking smile.

She should have been angry that he had taken such liberties, but she wasn't. It was im-possible to feel anything but the power of the attraction he held for her. There was a growing sense of alarm that she was giving in to him too easily, but even that had difficulty making itself heard.

His gaze focused on her mouth. "I think the coffee is the only thing around here that's getting cold." Unceremoniously, he kissed her before lifting her to her feet. "I'd better drink it and be on my way."

Jessica pushed a handful of hair away from her face and reached for her own cup. The coffee was lukewarm against her lips. She remained standing while Brodie drained his mug. Rising from the chair, he touched her cheek briefly.

"I'll call you."

"Yes." Jessica didn't walk him to the door. Brodie found his own way out of the apartment.

Chapter Seven

By Sunday night Jessica had almost convinced herself that she had succumbed to some temporary kind of madness. She had been kissed passionately before, had believed herself in love before, but her complete abandonment of control with Brodie had bordered on insanity.

Curled on the sofa, with her feet tucked beneath her, she closed the book she was holding. She hadn't read a single word in the past hour, and it was useless to pretend she would. It was equally useless to sit in the apartment. Maybe she should call her cousin Barbara Dane, her uncle's daughter, to see if she'd like go to a movie.

As she reached for the telephone sitting on the end table by the sofa, it rang. Her hand jerked back in surprise, then she picked up the receiver, wondering if Barbara had had the same idea.

"Hello?"

"I have a long-distance telephone call for Miss Jessica Thorne," the nasal voice of an operator responded.

"This is Miss Thorne," Her mind was racing. Her parents never called person-to-person this way. The only other person it could be was. . . .

"Hello, Green Eyes."

It was Brodie. Her heart did a somersault. "I thought you said you were going to call one day next week," she accused, but she couldn't stop the chills of delight from tingling through her.

"I said I'd make it back in town one day next week, but I didn't say I wouldn't call you in between," Brodie corrected. "What's the matter? Did I catch you at a bad time? Are you entertaining some amorous young man?"

"It so happens I'm alone." Her answer was snappish, a defensive mechanism as she wondered if Brodie thought she made a habit of behaving with all her dates as she had with him.

"All alone on a Sunday night?" He seemed to mock her solitude.

"I have to work in the morning," she reminded him.

"I forgot how conscientious you are. That's why you're having a quiet evening alone, isn't it?"

"Exactly why did you call?" Jessica demanded. "If it was just to make fun of me —"

"It's much more simple than that," Brodie interrupted. "I wanted to hear your voice."

Did he mean that? Jessica gasped back a sob as she realized that she desperately wanted him to mean it. He must have heard the strangled sound.

"Jessica?" His voice was crisp and inquiring.

"Yes?" Her tone was more subdued than it had been.

"I. . . ." There was a pause and she could

hear some background noises. "There's someone at the door. I'll have to let you go."

"All right. Goodbye, Brodie."

"Jessica . . . I'll call you." He sounded impatient, tired. Then there was only the hum of the dial tone as the connection was broken.

Slowly Jessica replaced the receiver on its cradle and hugged her arms around her stomach. She wished she understood him. She wished she knew whether she could trust him.

Monday, Tuesday, Wednesday went by while she waited for the promised phone call from Brodie. It didn't come. Jessica wondered whether her sharpness on Sunday had made him change his mind about seeing her again.

"One day next week," he had said. There weren't many days of the week left. Jessica stared resentfully at the office phone, its presence interrupting her concentration with a reminder of Brodie. It was probably a case of "out of sight, out of mind," and she should be glad of it.

The interoffice line buzzed. Jessica punched the button to the receptionist's desk and picked up the telephone. "Yes, Ann," she acknowledged the call. "What is it?"

"There's a Mr. Hayes on line one. Isn't he —"

But Jessica was already disconnecting the interoffice line to take Brodie's call. "Hello, Brodie." She hoped she didn't sound as eager as she felt.

"Hello, Jessica. I'm between meetings so I only have a couple of minutes." He sounded very brisk and coolly businesslike. "We can have dinner this evening."

"Tonight?" Jessica was all too irritatingly aware of the fact that he hadn't asked whether she had other plans.

"I'll come by your apartment at seven-thirty."

"I —"

"Sorry, Green Eyes, I have to run. See you tonight."

The line went dead. Jessica held the receiver away from her ear, glaring at it, impotent with the fury of being taken for granted. Her fingers were white from gripping the receiver.

"Jess?" The door to her office opened and her uncle, Ralph Dane, stuck his head inside. "Ann tells me that's Brodie Hayes on the phone. Tell him I'd like to talk to him for a few minutes."

"He's already hung up," she told him stiffly, and proceeded to do the same herself.

"Already?" A dark brow lifted in surprise. "That was a short conversation. Why did he call?"

"To tell me that I was having dinner with him tonight." Jessica bristled, unconsciously emphasizing the fact that she had been "told" and not asked.

Ralph Dane had been married many years and raised three daughters. He recognized the indignant look on Jessica's face and its cause. There was an attempt to hide a smile.

"Forgot to ask, did he?" His tone was sympathetic, but Jessica suspected that his sympathies were with Brodie.

"I'm beginning to suspect that Brodie Hayes never asks. He takes, commands, or presumes," she snapped.

"Don't be too hard on him, Jessie," her uncle attempted to mollify her. "At least you're assured that he wants to be with you and not someone else."

"Am I supposed to be grateful?" But she wasn't as sharp in her criticism as she had been a minute ago. There was consolation in knowing that Brodie wanted to be with her. "He could have pretended to observe the niceties of asking."

"You have to understand," Ralph Dane cautioned, "a man as successful as Hayes travels in a cutthroat circle. You have to be harder, tougher and stronger than the next man or he's going to step on you. There isn't much time for observing the niceties."

"Perhaps not," Jessica conceded, and remembered, also, that his upbringing had not permitted him to be as coached in good manners as she was.

"Tell him when you see him tonight that I'd like to talk to him about a couple of proposals Janson has made. I think he should know about them before I go ahead." The moment of family conversation had passed and her uncle was once again all business.

"I'll tell him," she promised.

By quarter past seven, she managed to rationalize away most of her irritation at Brodie's presumptuous behavior. Just enough of it lingered to put a combative sparkle in her eyes. She would have dinner with him, but she wasn't going to fall in his arms when he walked through the door.

The bell rang. Her pulse thundered erratically before she could bring it under control. Then taking a deep, calming breath, she smoothed her palm over the white silk of her dress and walked to the door.

"You're early," she said as she opened the door to Brodie. "You said you'd be here at seven-thirty and it's only a quarter after."

The glitter in his eye welcomed her into his arms, but Jessica turned away, refusing the invitation she read in his look. She swept into the living room, leaving him to close the door.

"Is it a crime to be early?" he challenged.

"I'm not ready yet." Which was a lie. She had been ready twenty minutes ago.

"Jessica?" His voice commanded and she obeyed by turning to face him. He made a thorough, disturbing study of her. "You look perfect to me."

All her senses were reacting to him, dangerously resplendent in his dark evening suit. "Thank you," she stiffly acknowledged his heady compliment, "but my lipstick —"

"Needs blotting." He caught her hand and pulled her into his arms.

She tried to keep her lips rigid under the slow exploration of his mouth, but a fiery glow of pleasure soon had them softening as her body relaxed in his hold. When Brodie lifted his head, he viewed her through the thick screen of his lashes.

"That's better," he declared.

Her gaze slid to his mouth and the beige pink smear of color. "You have lipstick on you now," she informed him, and moved out of his arms, clinging to the poise his kiss had all but shattered.

Brodie reached into his pocket for a handkerchief and proceeded to wipe away the telltale smear. "What's the matter, Jessica?"

"Nothing," she said.

"Yes, there is. Your nose is out of joint about something," he insisted.

Jessica was certain that nothing could remain hidden from those piercing blue eyes for long. "What if I told you I'd made other plans for tonight?" she challenged.

His gaze narrowed on her face, his look suddenly cutting and ruthlessly cold. "Have you?"

"It's a fine time to ask now, isn't it?" She laughed in brittle mockery.

Brodie caught her by the shoulders. Her dress was sleeveless and the minute his hands touched her, they began to lightly rub her soft

115

flesh. "If you'd told me —" he began with an attempt at patience.

"If you'd asked me," Jessica retorted, "I would have."

He expelled an angry breath. "How much time do we have before he shows up?"

Her eyes widened in hurt astonishment. He actually believed she was going out with someone else and he wasn't even jealous. Jessica didn't know whether to laugh or cry.

"All evening," she answered bitterly. "As it happens, I didn't have any plans for tonight, but you could have had the courtesy to ask." She glared at the knot of his tie. "I don't like being taken for granted, and I won't be at your beck and call!"

He forced her chin up, amusement glittering in his blue eyes. "I don't take you for granted, Green Eyes. At least, not consciously," he qualified his statement.

"I . . . I hope you don't." Jessica found it hard to stay angry.

Brodie reached inside his jacket. "Here, I bought you this." When his hand came out, it was holding a small narrow case. Jessica took it from him hesitantly, then lifted the lid. On a bed of black velvet was a delicate, spun-gold chain with a single, sparkling blue diamond.

"It's beautiful," she murmured, and felt her stomach twist into a sickening knot. She closed the lid and handed it back to him. "I can't accept it."

"Why not?" A dark eyebrow swept up in an arrogant, impatient line. "I bought it for you."

"It's much too expensive," said Jessica, fighting the waves of nausea. "I can't accept it."

"You're used to expensive things. Should I have bought you some cheap piece of costume jewelry and risked offending you?" Brodie demanded.

She lifted her head, her chin quivering with an abundance of pride. "At least I wouldn't feel as if you're trying to buy me."

"Buy you!" Brodie flared, and controlled his temper with effort. "I was not attempting to buy you."

"Do you make a habit of buying diamond necklaces for whatever girl you happen to be dating?" Jessica retorted.

"No, I don't make a habit of it," he denied with a savage bite. "I buy gifts only for people who are special to me. The motive is simple: I want to give them pleasure. That's all I get out of it, and that's all I expect to get out of it."

Perhaps he hadn't been trying to buy her affection. Jessica began to doubt the conclusion she had reached. She searched the tempered steel of his eyes.

"Then you shouldn't buy such expensive gifts and people wouldn't misinterpret your reasons," she backed down from her accusation.

"The cost is relative. I can afford this necklace." He lifted the case in his hand. "When I was fifteen, spending five dollars on a girl was a lot of money to me. Now I can afford to spend a great deal more." He studied her for a long second. "I want you to have this necklace, Jessica. Will you accept it?" She hesitated. "What good is money," he argued, "if you can't spend it on people you care about?"

His logic was irrefutable. Reluctantly she held out her hand for the case. "It was very thoughtful of you, Brodie." She recited her acceptance of it as if she was a child being prompted to say the right things. "It's beautiful. Thank you."

"Jessica," he sighed her name.

She lifted her gaze. Her green eyes were colored brightly with pride. A muscle flexed in his jaw where tanned skin was stretched taut. His hands closed over her shoulders, their hold firm but not gentle.

"I gave you that necklace with feeling," he said in a growling underbreath. "Why can't you put some feeling in accepting it?"

"I tried." Her answer was stiff as her body.

"You damned sure haven't tried hard enough." He hauled her against his chest. "It can be done without words."

His fingers wound into a handful of honey gold hair and forced her head back. The iron band of his arm crushed her ribs, denying her breath, while his mouth brutally smothered her lips. Jessica was caught in the dangerous whirlpool of his savage aggression.

She had angered him, aroused latent instincts from his childhood where survival and power went to the strongest. Despite the violence of his possession, her hammering heart was reacting to the indomitable force of his virility. She trembled at its power.

The sensuality of his kiss changed from punishment to passion. The iron bars of his imprisoning embrace became gloved in velvet, firm hands stroking her skin. Jessica experienced the exquisite joy of being mastered and responded to it. Then Brodie dragged his mouth from her lips to the pleasure spot behind her earlobe.

"We have so little time," he said in a groaning mutter, his breath hot and disturbing against her skin. "Do you want the necklace, Jessica?"

"Yes." She wanted anything from him — his anger, his kiss, his love.

It was a devastating discovery and she closed her eyes to hide it from him when he lifted his head. Her own was still tipped back, held there gently by the male fingers twined in her hair.

"Will you wear it tonight? Here?" His mouth located the hollow at the base of her throat.

"Yes," Jessica agreed, inhaling the earthy smell of him.

Brodie unwrapped his arms from around her and took the case from her hand. Snapping open the lid, he removed the necklace and Jessica watched the sparkle of the diamond come toward her. Obligingly, she lifted the curling length of hair at the back of her head so

Brodie could fasten the gold chain. Her skin tingled at the feather-light touch of his fingers.

When he took his hands away, she fingered the chain and the hard diamond nestled against her throat. Brodie turned her around so she could see herself in the wall mirror, but Jessica barely glanced at her own reflection before her eyes were drawn to his. He stood behind her, so tall and darkly compelling.

"It's beautiful," she told him. "I do like it."

"Do you?" The slant of his mouth was cynical in its mockery of her statement. "I much prefer your actions to your words. They're more convincing."

The sweep of his inspecting gaze made Jessica aware of her mussed hair and her mouth kissed free of any lipstick. She hardly resembled the poised, sophisticated woman Brodie had seen on arrival.

"You'd better go and fix yourself or the others will be guessing why we're late," Brodie taunted.

"The others?" Jessica echoed.

"Yes, that's my bad news for tonight. We won't be dining alone." He moved away from the mirror and Jessica turned to watch him.

"We're going to Janson's for dinner."

"You said 'others.' That sounds like more than two."

He lit a cigarette and blew a stream of smoke into the air. "I imagine there'll be a dozen in all

— Janson, his attorney, mine, my accountant, Janson's son."

"It sounds like a board meeting," Jessica commented.

"In a sense, it is." His mouth quirked. "Janson has been hounding me to come to his house for dinner, meet his wife, his family. There were a few details to iron out regarding the company. I combined business with a social obligation so I can have both of them out of the way at the same time."

"Actually you're ridding yourself of three obligations. You forgot me." Jessica smiled, but there was disappointment in knowing they would not be alone tonight.

"You're not an obligation, Jessica." He eyed her steadily, a faint grimness in his look. "When all this came up, I refused to deprive myself of the pleasure of seeing you again. I wanted to be with you . . . in the company of others if it couldn't be alone."

A searing pleasure coursed through her, sweetening the taste of disappointment. "I. . . ." The admission Jessica had been about to make suddenly made her tongue-tied, so she changed her response. "I'll only be a few minutes."

With her makeup freshened, her hair brushed into its style, and a silk shawl around her shoulders, she left the apartment with Brodie. On the way to the Janson home she remembered to relay her uncle's message, which drew a muttered exclamation of impatience from Brodie followed by silence.

The Janson home was a massive two-story structure with a porticoed entrance. Their host was at the door to welcome them and inform them that they were the last to arrive. As they were led into a formal living room, Jessica discovered she was nervous over the prospect of meeting Brodie's close associates.

Brodie made the introductions. Jessica shook hands with Drew Mitchell, a lean good-looking man who was Brodie's legal adviser, and his wife, Marian. Next was a balding man with black-rimmed glasses and a perpetually serious expression — Cliff Hadley, Brodie's financial consultant. After that was Janson's attorney, a smooth Southern gentleman named Lee Cantrel. His wife, Rachel, was an acquaintance of Jessica's, and several years older than she was. Finally there were young Cal Janson and his wife, Sue, and their hostess, Emily Janson.

When the introductions were completed, Cal Janson slapped Brodie on the shoulder. "It's time for a drink. I know you're a bourbon man, Brodie. How about the little lady here?"

"Sherry, please," Jessica ordered, knowing the older gentleman would be shocked if she asked for anything stronger.

Almost immediately the gathering became segregated into two groups: male and female. Brodie was off in the corner of the room with the men and Jessica was drawn into the circle of women.

"How are your parents?" Emily Janson inquired. "The community was so sorry to lose them when they sold their home and retired to Florida."

"They wanted to be near their grandchildren," Jessica explained politely.

"Of course, the climate there is marvelous. Cal and I usually spend a month or two there in the winter, but I could never persuade him to leave these Tennessee hills permanently."

The inconsequential chatter began, with Emily Janson portraying the perfect hostess, drawing each of the women into the conversation and leaving no one out. A short time later the dinner was served. Jessica found herself seated on the opposite side and at the opposite end of the table from Brodie.

She remembered, with irony, his comment that he hadn't wanted to deprive himself of the pleasure of seeing her. That was about all he was doing. Her gaze slid down the table to him. He was listening intently to something his attorney was saying in low tones. Jessica watched him rub his forehead, concentrating on the spot between his dark brows. But he didn't glance her way. She hadn't noticed him looking at her, so he hadn't been "seeing" much of her, either.

"How is Jordanna?" Rachel Cantrel inquired, sitting opposite Jessica at the long, formal dining table. "Are she and Tom still getting along together, or has the honeymoon finally ended?"

"Jordanna and Tom are very happy," Jessica answered calmly, but she was fiercely aware that the mention of her sister's name had drawn Brodie's attention when her presence hadn't.

The meal became an ordeal, the excellently prepared food tasting like chalk to Jessica. If her hostess noticed her lack of appetite, Emily Janson was too polite to comment on it.

After dinner, it was back into the living room for coffee and liqueurs. Again the men secluded themselves on one side of the room, embroiled in a business discussion, while the women sat on the opposite side.

Jessica sat on the plush sofa, a china cup and saucer balanced in her hand. From the sofa she could watch the men. Brodie rarely did any of the talking, his bland expression revealing none of his thoughts. Two or three times she noticed him briefly rub that one spot on his forehead. The gesture seemed to indicate that something serious was troubling him.

"Have you known Brodie long?" A voice inquired beside her.

Aware that she had been caught staring at him, Jessica turned to the woman seated on the sofa beside her. It was Marian Mitchell, the wife of Brodie's attorney.

"No, not very long," she admitted, and shifted the subject to the other woman. "Are you from here?"

"Gracious, no," the woman laughed. "We live

in Richmond — or we do when we're there, which is seldom. Since Drew started working with Brodie our home has become some place we *used* to live."

"How long has your husband worked for Brodie?"

"He's started his sixth year. I stopped counting how many airports we'd been in a long time ago or which hotels we'd stayed at." But Marian Mitchell didn't seem to be complaining.

"Don't you mind?" Jessica was curious.

"Drew loves working for Brodie. He enjoys the excitement, the feeling of never knowing what's going to happen next. The first three months I stayed home and saw Drew for a total of forty-eight hours. Our phone bill rivaled the National War Debt! I decided that I had a choice of living the life of a widow or packing my clothes and going with him. I've never regretted my decision to travel with him."

"Excuse me," Sue Janson interrupted their conversation. "It was very nice meeting both of you."

"Are you leaving?" Marian glanced up in surprise.

"Yes, we promised the sitter we would have her home by eleven, and it's after ten now," the young woman explained.

She said her goodbyes and entered the circle of men. It was several minutes before she was able to persuade her husband that they had to leave.

His departure made little impression on the other men, except as an unwanted interruption to their discussion. Emily Janson brought more fresh coffee.

Chapter Eight

It was after eleven. The four women had run out of small talk, but the men showed no signs of letting up. Jessica was quite certain they had forgotten they were in the room.

Marian Mitchell smothered a yawn with her hand and glanced at Jessica, Rachel Cantrel and their hostess. "This meeting will last until the wee hours of the morning — I've been through this before. Excuse me."

She walked to her husband, whispered something in his ear, and waited. Drew cast her an apologetic smile, then engaged in a hurried discussion with the others. Some sort of decision must have been reached, because Brodie separated himself from the group and walked over to where Jessica was seated.

He held out his hand for her to join him and nodded politely to the other two women. "Would you excuse us for a moment?"

"Of course," Emily Janson said with a smile.

Jessica's hand felt cold in the warm clasp of his as he led her into the large foyer. There was an absent look about him that said, even though he was with her, his thoughts were elsewhere. In the entry hall, he stopped.

"Drew is phoning for a cab to take Marian back to the hotel. I know you're tired and have to be at work in the morning. I don't know what time this meeting will break up, so I've asked Drew to arrange for the cab to take you home after it's dropped Marian at their hotel," Brodie informed her in crisply businesslike tones.

"That's very thoughtful of you," said Jessica, trying not to be offended that he was arranging to dispose of her like an inconvenience.

The touch of dryness in her voice narrowed his gaze. "I had no idea this was going to come up when I asked you to come with me this evening."

"I know that," she admitted. "And I know it must be very important to you."

"I'd take you home myself, but —"

"I quite understand, Brodie," Jessica interrupted.

His gaze flickered impatiently toward the living room. They still were in full view of the others, although their conversation couldn't be overheard.

"Do you understand?" he growled.

His hand closed roughly on her arm as he pushed her away from the living-room doorway. Seconds later she was backed up against a bare wall. Brodie leaned against her, an arm resting against the wall above her head, a hand cupping the side of her face. The crushing imprint of his body left her in no doubt of his true desire at the moment.

"Do you understand that all I want to do is

make love to you?" Brodie demanded before his mouth bruised her lips against her teeth.

Jessica was only allowed to answer by deed, returning the frustrated ardor of his kiss. Her hands explored his jaw and the column of his throat, nails digging into his shoulders. He rained angry kisses on her nose, cheek and ears.

"The problems aren't just mine," he explained, his voice muffled by her hair. "If they were, I'd say to hell with them. But it's those men in there. They have invested their time and talent in this project. I can't tell them to wait until I feel like handling the situation."

"I understand," she repeated, and she did, more fully this time.

"Hey, Brodie? Where are you?" Drew Mitchell called from the living room.

Brodie levered himself away from the wall and Jessica. A mask of control slipped over his features, changing his image from one of a passionate lover to a cool, poker-faced gambler. His indifferent blue gaze flicked to Jessica as if to be certain she was regaining control of herself. She had straightened from the wall. Brodie turned to the doorway.

"Out here, Drew."

The lean, brown-haired man rounded the corner. "Jessica's with you — good." He nodded. "The cab will be here in five minutes."

"Thanks, Drew." Brodie glanced at Jessica, his look still impersonal. "Will you be all right?"

She wondered what he would do if she said no. "Of course." She smiled, a tremulous action by a mouth that was still afire from his kiss.

There was barely time to say her goodbyes and thank her hosts for the evening before the taxi arrived. She waited while Drew kissed Marian. Brodie was already in the living room so they exchanged no tender farewell.

As the taxi pulled out of the driveway, Jessica leaned back in her seat and sighed, staring out the window into the blackness of the night.

"You'll get used to it," Marian said.

"Beg your pardon?" Jessica glanced at her companion.

"You'll get used to evenings ending like this if you continue seeing Brodie," the other girl explained her comment.

"Oh." Jessica couldn't think of anything else to reply.

"Like prices, all of Brodie's plans are subject to change without notice. Which means our plans, too. It's their way of life . . . Brodie's and now Drew's."

"Doesn't it bother you?" she repeated the question she had asked Marian earlier.

"If you love a man, you learn to accept the way he is and don't try to change him."

Jessica sensed the comment was meant as advice. "Yes, that's true," she agreed.

"Brodie is quite a man; all man. Who knows? Maybe if I'd met him before Drew, I might have fallen for him."

The woman was joking. Jessica sensed that Marian was very much in love with her husband. She had only made the comment to invite Jessica to confide in her. But Jessica wasn't sure enough of her own feelings to do that yet.

"Have you met Brodie's other girl friends?" she asked instead.

"Girl friends — that's the operative word." Marian seemed to consider the question. "I've seen him with other women, but he's never made a point of bringing them along for a social evening. I think I would have to say no, I haven't met his other girl friends. You're the first. Brodie generally keeps his private life private."

"I see." Jessica hadn't doubted for an instant that there were other women in his life, but it was a bit bolstering to hear Marian say that she was the first she'd met socially.

The cab whisked into the hotel entrance. Marian stepped out of the rear seat with a friendly goodbye, and Jessica continued the journey alone to her apartment complex.

At the office the next morning, a dozen red roses were delivered to her. The message written on the attached card had been simple. "I'm sorry. B."

All day long she had expected him to call. That night she sat by the telephone, but it didn't make a sound. Saturday morning, the operator called to read her a telegram, "Had to fly out of town. Be back next week," signed Brodie.

Jessica was beginning to discover what Marian had gone through when Drew was away so much. Not that she knew precisely. After all, Marian had been married to him at the time, whereas her own relationship with Brodie was tenuous at best.

On Wednesday night, the telephone was ringing impatiently when Jessica arrived at her apartment from work. She fumbled for the key and, in her haste, couldn't get it to turn the lock. An agonizing number of seconds went by before she could open the door and race to answer the phone.

"Hello?" Her greeting to the unknown party was eager and rushed.

"I missed you at the office. I called, but the girl said you'd just left." Brodie didn't bother with a greeting.

It didn't matter. Just the sound of his voice sent a thrill of happiness through her veins. "I just got home," Jessica admitted.

"After the last time, I thought I'd better call first to see if you'd made any plans for tonight." Brodie was dryly mocking.

"None," she told him shamelessly.

"I'll be over."

"When?" But the line was dead.

Jessica hung up the phone and glanced around the apartment. She hurriedly picked up the magazines scattered about, plumped the pillows and emptied the ashtrays. Then it was into her bedroom, out of her clothes

132

and under the shower.

Once out of the shower, she slipped into her short, Japanese-style robe. A shower cap had kept her hair dry. She brushed it until it glistened like gold, then began applying new makeup.

As she pressed a tissue to her mouth, blotting her lipstick, the doorbell rang. Jessica stared at her reflection in the mirror. It couldn't be Brodie, not yet. She wasn't dressed. There was nothing to do but answer the door. Wrapping the velour robe more tightly around her, she secured it closed with the sash, tying it in a double knot. Then she hurried to answer the second ring of the doorbell.

"I would have been here sooner, but I stopped to buy dinner." Brodie indicated the bag of groceries in his arm. His disconcerting blue gaze swept her from head to foot, noting the bare skin of her legs from her knees down and the V front of her robe fastened only by the tie around her waist. "I should have been here sooner," he corrected himself with a suggestive look that sent Jessica's pulse rocketing into space.

"I didn't expect you so soon." She moved out of his way when Brodie walked in. His lack of inhibition never ceased to remind Jessica of the abundance of hers. She closed the door behind him. "You can put the bag in the kitchen. It will only take me a few minutes to get dressed."

"Why bother?" In the short time it had taken

her to shut the door, Brodie had set the grocery bag on the nearest flat surface and was blocking her path.

"Brodie, please!" Jessica held up a hand to stave off his advance.

He used the obstacle to pull her into his arms. She strained against his hold, twisting her head to elude his mouth. But Brodie seemed to take pleasure in intimately investigating every inch of her exposed shoulder. The action sent delicious shivers of gooseflesh over her skin, all the way down until her toes curled. Weak with desire, Jessica let him capture her mouth, only to find his kiss more potent. She shuddered as his hands slid inside her robe and caressed the round globes that swelled to his touch, rosy nubs turning to hard pebbles under his teasing fingers.

When it seemed there was no turning back from the flames she sensed Brodie's withdrawal. The front of her robe was drawn closed and a last, hard kiss was planted on her lips. Then he was holding her away from him.

"There's a bottle of bourbon in the bag. Would you fix me a drink?" he asked huskily. "I'm going to need it."

Jessica opened her eyes slowly, hardly daring to believe that he meant it to end this soon. She wasn't even sure if she wanted him to stop now.

"I promised not to rush you, Green Eyes, so don't look at me like that unless you mean it." The smoldering light in his eye told her it wasn't an idle warning.

"I . . ." Jessica wavered, "I'll fix you a drink."

Brodie walked to the bag, handed her the bottle from it, then picked it up and followed her into the kitchen. "I thought we'd have dinner here tonight — it's the one place I can be sure there'll be no interruptions. Drew might guess I'm here, but since your number isn't listed he can't get hold of me." He set the bag on the counter while Jessica took a glass from the cupboard. "I hope you like steak."

His talking had given her time to settle her senses. She wondered if it had been deliberate on Brodie's part. There was so much about him that she was only just beginning to understand. He wanted her, but he was waiting until she could come to him with no regrets. His control of his emotions was frightening, as frightening as her lack of it.

"Yes, I like steak," she answered him.

"Show me where everything is." Brodie began unpacking the bag. "I'll do the cooking while you get some clothes on." He arched her a mocking look. "Imagine what your parents would think if they knew you were entertaining a man in your robe!"

Jessica ignored that. "Do you want your bourbon straight?"

"A splash of water and a couple of ice cubes will do."

She added two cubes of ice from the refrigerator and set the drink on the counter beside him. Unconsciously her hand moved to hold the gaping front of her robe together.

"It will only take me a couple of minutes to change. Have your drink. I'll take care of the cooking when I get back."

"I'll cook," Brodie insisted. "I'm very good. Don't forget I've led the life of a bachelor almost since I learned how to walk."

As it turned out, he was an excellent cook. The steaks were done to perfection, the new potatoes were steamed to lose none of their flavor. The sauce for the asparagus spears was creamier than Jessica had ever been able to make hers. Dessert was fresh strawberries.

Not only had the meal been superb, but so had the company and the conversation. They had talked about everything, argued over politics, agreed on musical tastes, had a few favorite authors in common. Over coffee, the subject had shifted to his business and the two men who worked so closely with him; his attorney and financial advisor — both of whom Jessica had met the previous week.

"Drew has practically become my right arm." Brodie swirled the half an inch of coffee left in his cup. "He's a very valuable man. I don't know how I got as far as I did without him."

The candlelight flickered and waned. The dancing flames drew Jessica's attention to the carved candleholders in the center of the table, the ones Brodie had bought for her. It seemed appropriate that they should be used for the first time with him.

"I think Drew has a great deal of respect and admiration for you, too," she commented.

"Why do you say that?" Their eyes met over the diminishing candles.

"Marian told me how much he enjoys his work, which has to mean that he enjoys working with you. That kind of feeling only comes when you respect and admire the other person. Besides —" she smiled "— he has to love his work or he wouldn't put up with the schedule you keep!"

"It gets hectic," Brodie admitted with a wry twist to his mouth. "You lose track of time and cities. All airports look alike."

Jessica noticed his cup was empty. "More coffee?"

"Please." He handed it to her in its saucer.

"Why haven't you ever married, Brodie?" she asked curiously, rising from the table to refill his cup.

"Who says I'm not?"

His reply hit her in the stomach. Shaken, she let go of the cup and saucer, which shattered on the floor. She clutched the back of her chair for support. Until that moment, it had never occurred to her that he might be married. Marian had said she'd seen him with other women, but she'd also said that he kept his private life private.

"You've broken the cup." Brodie rose from his chair and stooped to pick up the pieces.

Jessica stared at him. His hair gleamed blue black in the candlelight. The white of his shirt stretched across his broad, muscled shoulders and back.

When he straightened to hand her the broken pieces, she found her voice. "Are you?"

"Am I what?" A black brow arched in deliberate ignorance.

"Are you married?"

"Are you afraid you might be on the verge of having an affair with a married man?" he mocked the ashen color of her complexion, her eyes as green and round as the unbroken saucer. "It wouldn't be proper for a woman like you to become involved in a triangle like that, would it?"

Her fingers dug into the wooden back of the chair. "Answer me, Brodie! Don't play games."

"As it happens —" when she didn't take the pieces from him, he set them on the table "— I'm not married. Does that make you feel better?"

"Is that the truth?" Jessica continued to eye him warily, swallowing at the tightness in her throat.

"Don't you believe me?" he taunted softly.

"I don't know what to believe." She turned away, angry and frightened and uncertain. She crossed her arms, rubbing her hands over her elbows.

Silently Brodie came up behind her, his large hands closing around the soft flesh of her upper arms. "You can believe this." He kissed her neck.

Jessica lifted her shoulder to deny him access to her neck a second time, but he moved to the other side. She tried to twist away. Instead she was turned into his arms.

"And you can believe this." His mouth brushed her lips before she could turn them away.

"Stop it!" She kept her head lowered and turned to one side, but she didn't struggle.

"You're hurt and confused, aren't you?" His voice held amusement.

"Yes, damn you!" Jessica hissed.

The heat from his body was burning her skin, the muskiness of his male scent like a drug to her senses. She was aware how tantalizingly close his mouth was. All of these things stirred her blood.

"You're trembling," Brodie accused softly, "but not from anger. I can see that pulse beating in your throat. I make you feel things that you're not sure you should feel, especially with a married man. But if this is sinning, Green Eyes, imagine what heaven must be."

"Stop playing this cruel game!" She closed her eyes for a second, then opened them to give him a sideways glance. "Are you married or not?"

"I've already answered that question. Why should I repeat myself if you didn't believe me the first time?" he challenged with an arrogant

139

shrug. "I can't prove it. I don't carry around a piece of paper that says I'm unmarried, do you?"

"Of course not," Jessica answered impatiently.

"Then why should I believe that you're not married? Maybe you have a jealous husband lurking in some corner waiting to surprise us when we climb into bed, mmm?" He tucked a finger under her chin and turned it to face him, a wicked light dancing in his eyes.

"I don't think it's funny!" She flashed him an angry look.

"Neither do I. I hope to die in bed, but not by the hands of your husband," Brodie mocked.

"Stop it! You know I don't have a husband, jealous or otherwise," she snapped.

"What about me?" Brodie tilted his head to one side. "Look at me and tell me you think I have a wife tucked away somewhere."

Jessica lifted her gaze, but it faltered under his piercing stare, so sharply blue. She shook her head. "I can't."

"Then if I ask you to have dinner with me Saturday night, you'll accept?" He phrased it as a question.

The breath she released was a sign of surrender, unwilling but inevitable. "Yes, I'll accept," Jessica nodded.

"With feeling, Green Eyes," Brodie demanded.

Defiance flared as she looked up. "Damn you —"

She heard his throaty chuckle of triumph before his mouth descended on her vulnerable lips, parted in speech. They stayed that way under his direction. His hands moved to her hips, molding them tighter to his thighs. Her fingers, spread across his chest, slipped inside his shirt to tangle themselves in the froth of black hair.

"I have to leave, Jessica," he finally muttered against her mouth.

"Now?" Her breath was shaky, her lips trembling against the solid outline of his warm mouth. She couldn't believe he meant it.

"Yes, now." But his mouth refused to leave the corner of hers. "My plane is waiting for me."

"Again?" It came out in a moan of protest.

"I only flew in here to be with you tonight because I couldn't stay away a second longer."

Jessica could feel the disturbed pattern of his heartbeat. Not very different from her own. "I'm glad you did," she admitted.

His hands reached up to grip her shoulders and push her away from him. "If I leave now, I'll have just enough time to take a cold shower before we take off." He studied the glazed look of passion in her eyes. "Unless you want me to shower here . . . with you."

She hesitated, wavering between the yes of her flesh and the no of her mind. There was a cynical slant to his mouth.

"One of these days you aren't going to have to think before you answer, Jessica." He let go of her. "Saturday. Eight o'clock."

"Yes."

Chapter Nine

Saturday couldn't arrive too quickly for Jessica. She fluctuated between walking on air and dragging herself through the pits of depression. She spent half of her paycheck on a beige pant-suit that looked more like a pair of silk pyjamas, then worried how she would eat.

Marian's comment about Brodie's constantly changing plans had her listening for the ring of the phone. Pessimistically, she expected him to cancel their date.

Saturday night arrived and she was ready at seven. The mantel clock ticked away each second, all thirty-six hundred of them. This time Brodie didn't arrive early. He didn't arrive on time, either.

One minute after eight, Jessica began pacing the floor. She began imagining the reasons he might be delayed. Business, traffic, plane trouble. She glanced toward the phone, wondering if there had been an air crash.

Five minutes later she reached for the phone and the doorbell rang. She raced to the door and swung it open wide. Then she couldn't move, because Brodie was alive and unharmed.

"Don't you ever check first to see who's outside?" he smiled.

"I knew it was you."

One jacketed arm curved around her waist while the other pushed the door shut. Jessica's fingers slid along his lapel toward his neck. His hands locked behind her back, arching her to his length. The contact with his hard, muscled body seemed suddenly very intimate. The lines deepened around his mouth, suggesting that he knew exactly the upheaval he was causing to her fluttering heart and weakening knees.

"One of these days you're going to open that door to a stranger," Brodie warned. "You need a peephole installed."

"The apartment manager has been promising one," Jessica admitted.

While she looked up to his face, Brodie looked down to hers. The peephole was the farthest thing from her mind, but it was impossible to read what was written in his eyes. All she knew was that it was doing crazy things to her, like making her feel that she was wearing nothing beneath her pantsuit with its lacy, ribboned neckline, and she knew very well that she was.

"You're wearing the necklace I gave you," Brodie observed, but Jessica had the distinct feeling that his gaze was focused lower than the diamond at her throat.

"Yes." She felt out of breath and tried to control the rapid rise and fall of her breasts.

"No earrings. Is that an invitation to nibble?" He bent his head to gently take her earlobe between his teeth. The warmth of his breath

144

stirred all sorts of fires.

"I didn't have a pair that looked right." Desire throbbed in her voice.

It was a short side trip from her ear to her lips, but Brodie seemed to make it in record time. His mouth moved slowly in reexploring familiar territory, not ending the kiss until he had reinvestigated each curve and line of her lips.

"We can correct that," he said.

"Correct what?" What had been wrong? Jessica's quivering lips had found nothing wrong with the kiss. The only thing unsatisfactory about it was that it had ended.

Without answering, he reached into his inside pocket, his sleeved arm brushing across the front of her breasts. When he drew his hand out, it was holding a small square box. With a deft flick of his fingers, he snapped the lid open and a pair of diamond-studded earrings winked out at her, the brilliant gems as large as the solitaire of her necklace.

A cold chill ran down her spine, the same as before. She shook her head in a mute, negative rush of feeling. Her throat worked convulsively to ease the strangling constriction.

"Brodie, don't give them to me," she managed finally.

"It's a shame to break up a matched set, don't you think?" His arm at her waist made no attempt to hold her when she turned to walk away. "You'd better get used to accepting gifts

145

from me, Jessica, because you're going to get a lot from me. I'll never come to your door empty-handed."

Jessica glanced over her shoulder, her green eyes rounded and appealing in their confusion. His rough, compelling features were drawn in such grim lines. Why did he have to bring presents, she wondered. Because he had come empty-handed to her sister's door and been turned away? Didn't he realize that for her all he had to have in his hand was his heart? Perhaps he did. Perhaps he was giving her presents because he couldn't give her what she really wanted.

She controlled a shudder and offered a stiff, surrendering smile. "In that case, I'd better start learning to accept it now." But she wasn't referring to the gift.

When he walked over, Jessica removed the earrings from their jeweler's case and moved to the mirror to put them on. This time Brodie's reflection didn't join hers in the mirror and she faced him to receive his approval.

"How do they look?" Her brightness was forced.

"Beautiful." His response lacked emotion.

Standing there, with his feet slightly apart and a hand thrust into his pants pocket, he resembled a model out of the latest magazine of men's fashions. Smoke curled from the cigarette in his other hand. His rugged countenance was sternly masculine and forbidding in its expression of indifference.

Something inside Jessica shivered. "Are we ready to go?"

Over dinner, the atmosphere changed. Her apprehensions were temporarily forgotten under the spell of Brodie's charm. Again he became the companionable escort. They talked and laughed and discussed any subject. Not once was Jessica subjected to any of his mocking taunts. They seemed to come only when the air, or his thoughts, were heavy with passion.

It was nearly midnight when they paused at the door of her apartment. Brodie took the key from her and inserted it into the lock.

"Are you going to pretend to invite me in for coffee?" He pushed open the door and waited.

"Are you going to pretend to come in for coffee?" Jessica countered.

"Of course." His arm curved around her waist to guide her inside.

Closing the door, Brodie returned the key to her. Jessica dropped it in her bag and started toward the kitchen, but he caught her hand to stop her.

"Where are you going?"

"To put the coffee on."

"Pretend it's already on and we're waiting for it to be made." He kept a firm hold on her hand, drawing her with him as he walked to the sofa.

He sat down and pulled her onto his lap. He

wasted no more time on talk or preliminaries, his mouth unerringly finding hers in the dimness of the room. Her arms wound around his neck as she returned the slow-burning fire of his kiss.

All her nerves and senses were vibrantly alive and glowing under the golden heat of his kiss. Its warmth melted her inhibitions and a languorous passion was stealing through her bones.

His hand slid under the silky hem of her pantsuit top to reach her bare skin, setting her flesh on fire. With unhurried progress, his touch moved to the confining material of her bra. His fingers circled inside to cup the swelling roundness of her breast. A gasping sigh of sweet pleasure was muffled by his possessing kiss.

She was forced backward, onto the cushions of the sofa. Brodie followed her down, his length stretching partially on and beside her. His hands were stroking and molding her hips and thighs, arousing and satisfying the desire to fit her to every bruising contour of his body. A primitive need ached through her, a throbbing to have the expertise of his lovemaking brought to consummation.

"I want you, Green Eyes." Brodie nuzzled her neck, his voice thickened to a husky level. "For God's sake, don't say no!"

Jessica breathed in sharply, but it wasn't his request that was affecting her. His mouth had brushed her ear and she felt the cold metal of the diamond studs, precious gold and brilliant gems, so very expensive.

With a sudden twist she rolled away from him, stumbling upright to take a shaky step away from the sofa. She was hot with shame and a sense of degradation for the commitment she had almost made.

"I can't," she choked the denial. Her trembling fingers fought their way through the thickness of her blond hair to an earring. They made her feel like a mistress who had been rewarded in advance of pleasure given. "I . . . I feel as if I've been bought."

A pair of hands swung her violently around, sending the earring flying from her fingers. "Dammit, Jessica!" Brodie exploded with a fury that took her breath away. "We've been through that before!"

Nothing masked the fiery blast of rage in his eyes. "I . . . I know," Jessica stammered through her shock, intimidated by this profound display of emotion when she had almost believed him incapable of feeling anything deeply.

"The jewelry was a gift!" he snarled. "Not a payment for services!"

"I know." Her head bobbed in admission of what he had previously told her.

Brodie released his bruising hold of her shoulders with an obvious disdain. His carriage was rigid with anger as he stalked to where the earring lay, a sparkling treasure in the threads of the shag carpet. He picked it up and held it out to her.

"Here," he challenged, his tone icy.

Hesitantly, Jessica reached out and took it from his hand. She stared at the diamond, believing him and knowing she had accused him unjustly. Her conscience, her own sense of guilt, had caused the words.

"I'm sorry." She whispered the words, her head lowered, blond hair swinging forward to conceal her colorless cheeks.

He lifted her chin. "We'll have dinner next week. I don't know which night — I'll have to call you."

All she had to do was tell him not to bother and she knew she would never see him again. "Yes," she agreed, because the thought of not seeing him again was worse than the gifts she was loath to accept.

Holding her chin, Brodie pressed a cool kiss on her mouth. "Good night."

She murmured an answer as he walked to the door. He paused to send her one last look, his expression unreadable. Then the door was closing behind him.

During the next month Jessica saw Brodie at least once a week, sometimes twice. Always he brought a gift, a jade bracelet one time, a cashmere sweater another. Jessica never made any protest, accepting them and concealing, she hoped, the heaviness of her heart.

The sky outside the glass doors of her balcony was ink black. A crash of lightning illuminated trees whipped by the wind. The violent burst of light was followed by a roar of thunder that rumbled to shake the ground and rattle the glass in the windows. Rain lashed the panes, driven by a savage wind.

Jessica hugged her arms and turned her back on the fury of the spring storm. Brodie had called this afternoon to say he would see her tonight, but the rampaging weather was changing that. Incoming planes would be rerouted to other airports. He hadn't called her yet, but Jessica was sure he would when he landed safely elsewhere.

The doorbell rang. For a minute she stared at it in disbelief. Hesitantly she moved forward to answer it, opened it a crack, then swung it wide when she recognized Brodie. The dampness of his hair made it blacker still. His suit jacket was almost drenched by the rain.

"You didn't land in this weather!" Jessica protested.

Thunder rumbled. "It was a helluva flight, but it takes more than an act of God to keep me away from you," Brodie stated.

As he walked into the apartment, she saw how haggard he looked. The last two times she had seen him, she had noticed he seemed tired. Tonight, exhaustion had carved deep lines in his face, even dulling the sharpness of his eyes.

"Your jacket is wet. You'd better take it off."

She stepped behind him to help him with it.

"Your present is in the inside pocket," he told her when she draped the sodden garment over a chair back.

Her hand hesitated on the damp material. "I'll get it in a minute." She glanced over her shoulder to see him tiredly rub the back of his neck. "How about a drink?"

"Sounds good."

The storm had broken shortly after six o'clock. Jessica had been so certain that Brodie wouldn't be able to make it that she hadn't bothered to dress. She was wearing the tight-fitting brushed denims and red chambray blouse that she'd put on after work. The storm, her clothes and his tiredness convinced her that the place to have dinner was in her apartment.

As she fixed his bourbon and water, Brodie called from the living room. "Do you mind if I use your phone? I have to get hold of Drew."

"Go ahead," she answered.

When she returned to the living room, Brodie was seated on the sofa. He was leaning forward, his elbows on his knees, holding the telephone receiver with one hand and rubbing his forehead with the other. Jessica set the drink on the table beside him and his mouth quirked briefly in thanks. His attention was instantly back to the phone.

"Hello, Drew. It's Brodie."

The line crackled. Then his attorney's voice came through so clearly that Jessica could hear it. "Brodie! Where the hell are you? I've been trying to reach you for the last two hours."

"I'm in Chattanooga."

"Chattanooga?" The stunned response echoed into the room. "That's the fifth or sixth time you've made an unscheduled stopover there. Listen, if you have to keep holding Janson's hand, maybe we have the wrong man for the job. What the hell's the problem this time?"

Brodie leaned against the sofa back and attempted to loosen the knot of his tie. Jessica reached over and did it for him, unfastening the top three buttons of his shirt.

"I'm not here to see Janson."

"Then what are you doing there?" In the pregnant pause that followed Drew's question, Brodie glanced at Jessica. She wondered if he would respond to that invasion of his privacy. But the need didn't arise as Drew guessed, "You're there to see Jessica, that blonde you took to Janson's place. Brodie, I know I'm butting my nose in where it doesn't belong. You're as human as the next man. If you have to keep making these stops in Chattanooga, rearrange things. You're beating yourself to death with this schedule."

"That's my worry, not yours." There was just enough snap in his voice to terminate that discussion. "I went over those figures Cliff gave me on the food-processing plant in Memphis, and they told me nothing. I'll be there in the morning. Have Cliff meet me at the airport with something more than what I have."

"What time?"

"What time am I supposed to meet the banker in Nashville?" Brodie countered.

"Nine, I think. Yes, nine o'clock."

"Okay, change it. Have Cliff fly to Nashville. Take the earliest flight. That way I can go over everything with him en route to Memphis. Anything else?"

"It can wait until I see you tomorrow," Drew answered.

"All right, see you then." Brodie hung up.

"He's right, you know," Jessica said. "You are working too hard." She reached out to lightly trace the deep groove near his mouth with her fingertips.

"I am, huh?" He caught her hand and pulled her over to kiss her hand. Then with a reprimanding slap on her rump, he pushed her away. "Go and open your present."

Jessica walked over to the chair where his jacket was. "I thought we'd have dinner here tonight instead of going out, is that all right?" It was easier to talk about something else while she was opening the package she didn't want.

"Perfect." His hooded gaze watched her strip away the paper.

"How hungry are you?" Her mind raced through the contents of her cupboards, trying to plan a menu.

"Ravenous. I don't think I've eaten since yesterday."

"How could you forget something like that?" she laughed, and tried to ignore the box in her hand.

"It's easy. I could have had something on the plane tonight, but I knew I'd be having dinner with you, so I waited."

There was no way to delay opening the box any longer. Inside was a gold cigarette lighter with the letter *J* etched on it, the initial punctuated with a diamond.

"It's beautiful." Jessica admired it for the necessary minute, then walked over to kiss him. "Thank you." She tasted the bourbon on his mouth. "Is the drink all right?" she said, changing the subject as quickly as she could.

"Very good. And very thoughtful."

"Just trying to show a little old-fashioned Tennessee brand of hospitality." She smiled. "You sit back and enjoy your drink. I'll start dinner."

Her choice of menu was limited by the food and the amount of it on hand. It turned out to be more Italian in origin than Tennesseean, with a salad, spaghetti and meat sauce, and warmed bread. But it was quick and hot and stuck to the ribs. Afterward Jessica cleared the table but left the dirty dishes in the sink to join Brodie in the living room.

"Would you like another cup of coffee?" she asked.

"Not particularly." Seated on the sofa, he was looking at her in a most disturbing way. "Drink, dinner, more coffee — are you trying to impress me with your hospitality?"

Outside the thunder and lightning were still competing for honors in a violent contest. Jessica was indifferent to the battle. It was happening on the periphery and had little to do with them.

"Come here," Brodie ordered, and lazily watched her cross the room to stand in front of him.

Pulled onto his lap, Jessica met his kiss halfway, her lips parting almost instantly to know the full possession of his mouth, sensual and stimulating. His hands tugged her blouse free of her waistband and began unfastening the buttons.

Abandoning herself to the heady oblivion of his kiss, she could only think of the pleasure her flesh would feel at his touch. His fingers entered the shadowy valley between her breasts.

His mouth curved against her lips. "It must have been a man who invented bras that hook in front."

In the next second, her breasts were freed of their enslavement. Brodie's mouth burned its way down her throat to celebrate their release. Her fingers curled into the springy thickness of his black hair, her hands pressing his head to her. A sweet ecstasy claimed her at his intimate caresses. Eventually his mouth returned to her

156

throat and neck, taking sensuous little nibbles of her skin.

"Isn't this better than coffee?" Brodie mocked her when she couldn't hold back a tiny moan of desire.

"Much better," she admitted in a disturbed whisper.

"Now if you're really intent on showing me your hospitality, you'd offer me a place to sleep." He teased her mouth, making it tremble for his kiss.

"I do have —" she tried to end the tantalizing brush of his lips, but he continued to elude her "— a spare bedroom."

"If I stayed, you know I wouldn't sleep there."

His hand was at her waist and the snap of her jeans gave way to his probing fingers. The telephone rang at the same instant. Jessica jumped guiltily at the sound. She heard Brodie's muffled curse as she leaned over to reach the telephone on the end table beside the sofa.

"Hello?" Jessica avoided glancing at Brodie as she answered the phone.

"Is Brodie there? Let me speak to him," an unfamiliar male voice requested.

Covering the mouthpiece with her hand, Jessica looked questioningly at Brodie. "It's for you." There was a disconcerting darkness to his pupils, ringed with clear blue.

His mouth thinned grimly. "Find out who it is."

She took her hand away from the telephone. "Who's calling, please?"

"Tell him it's Jim. I just got an update on the weather," the voice answered.

Jessica covered the receiver again and relayed the answer. "It's a man named Jim. Something about the weather."

"I'll take it." Brodie took the receiver from her hand and helped her off his lap. "Yeah, Jim. What's the word?"

Jessica couldn't hear the reply as she turned away from Brodie to fasten her bra and button her blouse. There was a shaking awareness of how much she wanted Brodie to make love to her. At the moment, the desire was drifting into the past tense under the brilliant light of uncertainty. She guessed that he had only to touch her again and the light would go out.

"Okay, Jim, I'll be there." Brodie hesitated a minute, then replaced the receiver.

"Who is Jim?" Jessica asked, pushing her hair away from her face.

His gaze flickered over her buttoned blouse front. "My pilot. Radar shows this storm cell should be out of the area in about a half an hour. There's another one approaching that should arrive in an hour, possibly an hour and a half. If we expect to take off tonight, it has to be soon."

"Your pilot? You mean you have your own plane?" Jessica stared.

"A little Lear jet."

"A little Lear jet?" She laughed in astonishment. "I thought . . . I guess I thought you were flying in and out on a commercial line . . . or a charter. I didn't realize you owned your own plane, complete with a crew."

"I'll take you for a ride in it some day," he promised, faintly amused by her reaction. "I'll have to leave. I'll probably be back next Tuesday." He rose from the couch.

Jessica looked up. "I'll be waiting."

Brodie curved a hand around the back of her head and bent down to kiss her. It was brief and unsatisfying for both of them. When he straightened, she reached out for him, but he was already striding toward the door.

Chapter Ten

On Tuesday, a meeting at the office made Jessica late returning to her apartment. She hurried along the corridor, hoping she'd have time to shower and relax before Brodie came. At the door, she blew a strand of hair from out of her eyes and inserted the key in the lock.

But the door wasn't locked. Jessica was positive she had locked it this morning when she had left. Cautiously she pushed the door open and glanced inside. The first thing she noticed was the aroma of roast beef. She frowned. Was Brodie here? Had he arrived earlier and persuaded the manager to let him in?

Walking inside, she closed the door. "Hello?" she called.

A girl stuck her blond head around the corner of the kitchen. "Well, it's about time you got home."

"Jordanna!" Jessica stared at her sister. "What are you doing here?"

"Surprise!" was the laughing response. "Tom and I are on vacation. Mom and dad volunteered to look after the children. So here we are, two weeks all to ourselves!"

Before Jessica could recover from the shock, she was being hugged by her older sister. "But what are you doing here?"

"We're on our way to Memphis to see Justin, then on to New Orleans to spend time with Tom's parents. We decided to spend the night here with you. It will give us a chance to visit. Gracious, we haven't seen you since Christmas," her sister declared, stepping back to take a look at her. "You seem different, changed." Green eyes, a shade brighter than Jessica's, glittered with knowledge. "It must be a man."

Jessica's mouth became dry. "There is someone," she admitted reluctantly.

"You'll have to tell me all about him. Come in the kitchen with me." Jordanna took hold of her hand and pulled her toward the room. "I was just going to add some carrots and potatoes to the roast."

"I . . . I was going to take a shower. It's been a long day and —"

"Tom's using it now." Her sister, unknowingly, cut off that avenue of escape. Cleaned carrots and potatoes were sitting in a colander in the sink. When Jessica reached for them, her sister protested, "Pour yourself a cup of coffee and sit down. I'll take care of dinner."

Jessica did as she was told and watched Jordanna open the oven door, releasing a new wave of cooking smells. It was the first time she had really looked at her sister in years. Motherhood and maturity had affected her figure, which was still trim but now bordered on the voluptuous. Her hair was rinsed to a platinum shade and styled in a short, youthful cut that framed her attractive oval face and drew attention to her unusual green eyes. Fresh and outgoing, her personality was one of Jordanna's greatest assets. Jessica felt her heart sinking.

"How are the children?" she heard herself ask.

"Fine. Julie has to wear braces on her teeth, which infuriates her. I can remember. . . ."

But Jessica didn't bother to listen to the rest. She was wondering where Brodie was and whether there was any way she could get in touch with him to let him know that she couldn't go out with him tonight. Somehow she had to prevent him from coming, but she didn't stop to consider her motive.

"Jessica, did you hear me?"

Startled, she looked up. "I'm sorry. I guess I was daydreaming. What did you say?"

"It doesn't matter," Jordanna laughed, a pleasant, warm sound. "Who is this new man in your life? Anyone I know?"

"He'd better not be," a familiar voice declared from the doorway as Tom Radford walked into the kitchen, saving Jessica from answering the question. She hadn't mentioned Brodie to any of her family except her uncle. She wasn't sure what their reaction would be, especially her sister's. "Hello, Jessica. You're looking more beautiful each time I see you," Tom greeted her.

"I think that's because she's in love," Jordanna teased.

"I do believe she's blushing," Tom observed, joining his wife to gang up on Jessica.

Deliberately she ignored both remarks. "It's good to see you again, Tom," she greeted her brother-in-law, a tall, good-looking man with brown hair and a few extra inches around his waistline. "Even if I wasn't expecting you. When I discovered the door unlocked I almost called the police. I thought someone had broken into my apartment," Jessica lied.

"It was Jordanna's idea; I wanted to call to let you know we were coming, but she thought it would be more fun to surprise you," he explained.

"It certainly was a surprise," she admitted. "Does Justin know you're coming?"

Jordanna explained that they were going to surprise her brother, too. Then Tom related their plans for New Orleans, the sight-seeing they were going to do, and the relatives they were going to visit. Jessica felt the minutes ticking away, yet she still wasn't able to think of a way to contact Brodie.

"Do you have any bay leaves, Jessica?" Her sister was opening cupboard doors, looking for spices.

"The one on the left side of the sink," Jessica directed.

But Jordanna paused at the adjoining cupboard. "There's a bottle of bourbon here. Can you believe that, Tom? My baby sister has liquor in her cabinets!"

"I've grown up, Jordanna," she responded patiently.

"You certainly have," Tom agreed. "And there's absolutely nothing wrong with good bourbon. Fix me a drink, wife," he ordered.

"How're mom and dad?" Jessica asked to change the subject.

"Fine. Tom took dad out golfing with him in January, and now dad has the bug. He has his own set of golf clubs and he's talking about buying a golf cart," Jordanna answered as she opened more cupboards until she found the glasses.

Jessica's nerves were stretched to breaking point as she listened to her sister tell about the seat cushions their mother was needlepointing for the dining-room set. It all seemed so unimportant.

The doorbell rang. Jessica's heart leaped into her throat. "I'll get it," she mumbled, and had to fight her trembling knees to make it into the living room.

This time she didn't open the door wide to Brodie. She opened it a foot and blocked his entrance. Her complexion was pallid, her breathing shallow. She had difficulty meeting his curiously inquiring gaze.

"Something's come up, Brodie. I'm afraid I can't go out with you tonight," Jessica rushed, keeping her voice low.

A frown darkened his rough features. "What is it? What's wrong?" His hand came up to push at the door. For a minute, she tried to hold it before realizing she was no match for his strength.

"Nothing's wrong. It's just that I have some unexpected company," she explained as he stepped inside the doorway. "I would have let you know, but I —"

"Jessica, do you have any mushrooms?" Jordanna walked into the living room and stopped abruptly.

Brodie's gaze swung to her, his expression slowly lightening into a smile of recognition. Jessica watched the transformation and felt sick inside.

"Jordanna! It doesn't seem possible, but you're more beautiful than I remembered," he said, his voice husky and caressing.

"Brodie?" Jordanna stared at him uncertainly, her head tipped to the side. "Brodie Hayes? It can't be!"

"But it is." He walked forward to take her hand and carry it palm upward to his lips, a gesture that came as naturally as shaking hands. "After all these years, I thought you would have forgotten me."

Jessica watched the pleased smile that spread over her sister's face at Brodie's open display of admiration. There was no sign of nervousness or feelings of intimidation. In fact, Jordanna looked quite attracted to him.

"I haven't forgotten you," Jordanna assured him. Neither of them appeared to notice Jessica standing several feet away, excluded from their reunion. "How have you been? Where have you been? What have you been doing?" She rushed with a sudden need to know everything about him.

"Jordanna, I found the mushrooms for you." Tom walked around the corner and stopped when he saw his wife with a strange man. "Hello." He didn't look the least bit upset, not even by the fact that Brodie was still holding Jordanna's hand.

"Did you ever meet my husband, Tom?" Jordanna asked with absolute unconcern. "Tom, this is Brodie Hayes. My husband, Tom Radford."

"I don't believe we've met." Brodie released Jordanna's hand to shake Tom's. "How do you do, Tom."

"I take it you're an old friend of Jordanna's," he said, smiling.

"That's right." He cast a look sideways at Jordanna. "I tried very hard to make it more than friendship, but she already had you in her sights at the time."

Jessica wanted to scream and stamp her feet and tell them all that Brodie was here to see her. The trouble was he had lost interest in her the minute he'd seen Jordanna. It was the very thing she had feared all along, only she had refused to face it.

"What are you doing here?" Jordanna asked curiously.

But it was Tom who put two and two together. "Are you the mysterious man in Jessica's life?" he joked.

"Oh!" Jordanna clasped a hand over her mouth in surprise. "Are you dating Jessica?"

"Yes, as a matter of fact, we were supposed to have dinner together tonight." For the first time since he'd seen Jordanna Brodie glanced behind him to Jessica. It seemed like an invitation to join the circle. She walked stiffly forward, pride refusing to let the hurt show through. "Only now she tells me it's off."

"Jessica, you don't have to cancel your date just because we're here." Tom frowned.

"But you're only going to be here tonight. When else would I have a chance to talk to you?" Jessica rigidly defended her action.

"We never meant to upset your plans, Jessica," her sister apologized. "Stay for dinner, Brodie. I have a roast in the oven. There's plenty for all of us."

"No!" Jessica spoke without thinking how it sounded. She was conscious of Brodie's piercing gaze narrowing on her. With difficulty, she met it. "I know how busy your schedule is. I'm sure there's some place you have to be other than here."

"I took Drew's advice and rearranged my schedule so it wouldn't be so crowded," he told her. "There isn't any place I have to be until tomorrow afternoon."

"Well, I'm sure there are papers or financial statements you need to go over," Jessica tried to find a reason for him to leave.

"A man can't work all the time," Tom inserted. "Stay for dinner, Brodie."

"It seems you're outnumbered, Jessica," said Brodie, measuring her with a cool look. "That's two invitations for dinner."

"You're welcome to stay, of course," she lied. She wanted him far away from here . . . and from her sister. "I just thought you might have something more important to do."

"Not a thing. I'm glad you want me to stay." A muscle jumped in his jaw as he uttered the last statement in a faintly sarcastic tone.

"How did the two of you meet?" Jordanna questioned, missing the charged look that passed between Brodie and her sister.

"I picked her up on a street corner about two months ago." Brodie phrased it so it was deliberately suggestive. When he saw the fire flash in Jessica's eyes, he smiled. "We bumped into each other quite by accident. When I first saw her I thought it was you, Jordanna. It was only after a few minutes that I realized the resemblance was superficial."

Jessica wanted to die — that he should actually admit he had mistaken her for her sister. It seemed the final humiliation.

"Excuse me," she murmured. "I think I'd

better check on the dinner."

She retreated into the kitchen. Jordanna, despite her earlier protestations that she would fix it, stayed in the living room with Brodie and Tom. She could hear them talking and laughing. Jealousy seethed through her veins.

The roast was out of the oven when Jordanna finally wandered in to help her. Jessica barely glanced at her as she took a meat platter from the cupboard to put the roast on. At that moment, she was trying very hard not to hate her sister.

"The table is already set," Jessica told her. "You can get a bowl down for the potatoes and carrots."

If Jordanna noticed her waspish tone, she ignored it. "Brodie has certainly done well for himself, hasn't he?" she murmured as if speaking her thoughts aloud.

"Yes. Do you want to make the gravy or shall I?" Jessica didn't want to discuss Brodie with her sister.

"I will. Where's the flour?" Jordanna asked, and opened the cupboard Jessica pointed to. "He's really a very attractive man."

"You didn't used to think so," Jessica reminded her. She didn't give her sister a chance to reply as she carried the platter of meat to the table in the dining room. "Will you slice the roast, Tom?" she requested, and avoided looking at Brodie.

The meal was a miserable ordeal, listening to

Jordanna and Brodie talking about the past. Tom had been a part of it, so he joined in the conversation. Jessica hadn't, and she wasn't a part of the dinner conversation, either. She was the fifth wheel and felt it all the way to her bones. She served the dinner, cleared the plates, brought the dessert and coffee, and was as ignored as a servant.

"It hardly seems that long ago, Brodie," Jordanna sighed as she took the photographs she had shown him of her children and put them back in her purse. "Yet I have two children who aren't that much younger than we were when you came to my house wanting me to go for a ride with you."

"Yes, and you turned me down flat," Brodie recalled dryly. "I was the boy from the wrong side of town. It isn't surprising that you didn't want anything to do with me."

"I don't know." Jordanna seemed to consider the thought. "Where you came from didn't have much to do with it. If I hadn't already met Tom, I probably would have accepted your invitation."

Jessica didn't want to hear this. She rose abruptly from the table. "Excuse me. I think I'll wash the dishes."

"We can do them later, Jessica," Jordanna protested.

"I'd rather do them now," Jessica insisted tightly. "It's getting late and I —"

"Jessica's right. It is getting late," Brodie inserted. "I've intruded on your family gathering long enough. It's time I was leaving." He rose from the table and glanced pointedly at Jessica.

Courtesy demanded that she offer, "I'll see you to the door."

"Thank you." There was dry mockery in his voice. He took hold of her arm as if he expected her to change her mind and was determined that she would follow through with her offer. Jessica stood rigid in his grasp while Brodie made his good-nights to her sister and brother-in-law.

There was an electric quality to the air when they reached the door. Her features were frozen in a smooth mask of ice. Its thickness withstood Brodie's attempt to penetrate it. He reached in his pocket and took out a long, thin case.

"Here. I didn't have a chance to give it to you earlier," he said.

Jessica's fingers curled around the gift. She longed to throw it in his face or tell him to give it to Jordanna, but this late in the evening, she was well schooled in controlling her emotions.

"It's a strand of pearls," Brodie told her when she made no attempt to open it.

"I'll open it later. Thank you." A poor replica of a smile curved her stiff mouth.

His jaw hardened, his nostrils flaring in anger. Then his gaze flicked to the adjoining room and the couple who were doing their best to ignore the two at the door.

"I'll call you," he said, and it sounded like a threat.

Jessica briefly inclined her head, but Brodie wasn't looking. He was opening the door and walking out, closing it behind him much too quietly. Jessica shuddered and turned away.

"Has he left already?" Jordanna asked the obvious. "What's that in your hand? A present?"

"Yes." Jessica stared at it. Her fingers were as white as the paper it was wrapped in.

"Well, open it. Don't you want to see what it is?" her sister urged, coming into the living room to join her. To make a negative reply would have invited questions Jessica didn't want to answer. Unwillingly she tore the paper off and opened the box. "Pearls!" Jordanna exclaimed. "They're beautiful!"

"Is it some special occasion or something?" Tom asked.

"No, no special occasion." Jessica looked at the perfect strand of matched pearls, but couldn't bring herself to touch them. "Brodie just does this."

"Lucky you." Her sister smiled, then turned to her husband to scold him playfully, "How come you never bought me presents like that when we were dating?"

"I didn't want to spoil you. Besides —" Tom glanced at the pearls, his look assessing "— I wasn't rolling in money the way he is."

After that, Jessica was besieged by questions about Brodie, some of which she dodged, others she answered. It was a relief when the hour grew late enough that she could escape them to the isolation of her room. The bed was inviting, but sleep was far away.

In the morning, Jessica was able to pretend that she was sorry to see her sister go. She even managed to lie that she wished Jordanna could stay longer.

An hour after Jordanna and Tom had left for Memphis, Jessica was at the office, tormented by the hell of being jealous of her own sister. A tight ball of nerves, nothing she did went right. By ten-thirty that morning she was bent over her desk, her face buried in her hands. She was certain she was losing her sanity and wondered how she would get through the rest of the day.

The door to her office opened and Brodie walked in, tall and vigorous while she felt small and beaten. She stared at him, half-afraid she was having hallucinations.

"What are you doing here?" she breathed.

"I came to take you to lunch," he said, matter-of-factly.

"But you said last night that you had an appointment at noon."

"Yes, I do, in Nashville. We're flying there for lunch. I promised you a ride in my jet, remember?" An eyebrow lifted, arrogant and mocking, yet his look was piercing.

"But I can't —"

"Yes, you can," Brodie interrupted her protest. "I've already spoken to your uncle, and he has no objection if you take a few hours off. The lost time of a minor assistant is negligible compared to the large advertising account of Janson Boats. Get your handbag. We don't have much time."

Jessica was swept into the maelstrom of his commanding presence. Before she could think, she was hustled out of the office, into his waiting car, and was halfway to the airport. By then it was too late. She stared at the clasped hands in her lap and wondered what kind of fool she was.

"I presume Tom and Jordanna left early this morning."

"Yes, they did," she acknowledged stiffly.

He shot her a piercing glance. "Why were you so anxious to get rid of me last night, Jessica?"

She started guiltily. "Don't be ridiculous! I wasn't anxious to get rid of you," she lied. "I know the way you drive yourself. I thought you'd be better off resting than listening to a lot of boring family conversation."

"I wasn't bored."

No, Jessica swallowed at the pain that knifed through her, Jordanna didn't bore him. Her sister never had. She felt his glance and knew she had to make some response.

"I'm glad," she murmured as he parked in front of an airplane hangar.

The sleek private jet was waiting on the concrete apron. There were hurried introductions of Jessica to the pilot, Jim Kent, and the copilot, Frank Murphy, before she was hustled aboard.

The interior of the aircraft was not fitted out for passenger seating, but instead resembled a den with two lightweight desks mounted to the floor, some comfortable-looking chairs and a divan. Brodie helped her to buckle herself into one of the chairs.

"Have you ever flown before?" He took a seat near her.

"Yes, but never in anything like this." The plane was rolling down the runway. Jessica could feel the acceleration of the powerful jet engines.

"It's very practical. There's work space for myself and Cliff or Drew. There's a shower in the washroom." He continued to talk to her as the plane roared into the air. "I can nap on the divan. There're facilities for drinks and snacks."

Jessica glanced at him. "Are you trying to impress me?"

"Are you impressed?" Brodie countered, his mouth quirking.

"Yes," she admitted.

"Good."

"How long will it take to get to Nashville?"

"It's a short flight. By the time we take off, climb to the designated altitude, and level off, Jim starts his descent." He was eyeing her with an intent yet rather mocking look. "There isn't enough time to earn a 'mile-high' pin."

"What's that?" she asked blankly.

"That, Green Eyes," Brodie unfastened his seat belt and straightened to tower beside her, "is given when you've made love a mile above ground."

His low, throaty laugh said that he had noted the agitated movement of her breasts. His hand cupped the back of her head, turning her face up. There was the blinding brilliance of his gaze on her. Then he was kissing her long and hard, eating away her resistance with his devouring mouth. Jessica responded, convinced she was without pride where Brodie was concerned. When he straightened, she felt light-headed and shaken.

"Want anything to drink?" he offered. "Coffee? Tea?"

Or you, she thought.

"Nothing," she refused.

While he got himself some coffee, she sat quietly in her chair. She found herself wondering how many women had received a "mile high" pin from him. Her stomach churned in a sickening knot.

A rental car was waiting at the Nashville airport. They lunched with some stranger. Afterward Brodie drove her back to the airport and put her on his jet alone to be flown back to Chattanooga.

"I'll call you next week," he told her as he kissed her goodbye.

She would be waiting. She had the feeling she would always be waiting.

Chapter Eleven

Brodie didn't call. A week later he drove up to the curb of her apartment building just as Jessica was arriving home from work. He honked the horn to call her over and left the engine running.

"Shall we go for a ride?" he asked.

"All right. Give me a couple of minutes to change."

"There's nothing wrong with what you're wearing." His gaze swept over the dirndl skirt and beige blouse she had on.

"But I —"

"Are you looking for compliments?" The slant of his mouth taunted her.

"No," Jessica denied.

"Then climb in," he ordered. When she was in the passenger seat and the door was closed, Brodie shifted the car into gear and turned it onto the street. His gaze glittered to her briefly. "Are you upset with me for not calling?"

"I . . . no," she admitted. As long as she saw him, it didn't seem to matter whether she knew in advance or not. And that was the shameless truth.

As if he knew what the admission had cost her in pride, Brodie took hold of her hand, linking his fingers with hers and carried the back of her hand to his mouth. Her hand remained in the warm clasp of his as he drove through the city streets. Jessica leaned against the seat, turning her head on the back rest to study his profile. She felt she had been more than amply rewarded for telling the truth.

"Have you had a rough week?" He didn't look tired, at least not as tired as he had that other time he had visited.

"Not any more than usual." Brodie slowed the car to make a sharp turn onto a tree-lined road.

"Where are we going?" Jessica glanced around, noticing that they had seemed to leave the city behind.

"I forgot. Your present is in the glove compartment," he said. Hiding her displeasure, Jessica opened the compartment. There was an envelope inside with her name on it. She hesitated. Surely he wouldn't be so crude as to give her money? "Go on, open it," Brodie prodded.

Grudgingly she took it out and lifted up the flap. There was a key inside. Her gaze flew to Brodie as she held it up. "What's this for?"

He merely smiled, made another turn, and slowed the car to a stop. As he switched off the engine he glanced to her. "Why don't you try it on that door?" he suggested, and nodded in the direction behind her.

Jessica turned. They were parked in the driveway of a sprawling house nestled on the crest of a hill. A thousand questions spun through her mind, but a second look at Brodie told her he would provide the answers when he felt it was time.

She climbed out of the car and waited for Brodie to join her. Together they followed the curving sidewalk to the front door. The key in her hand turned the lock. She glanced at Brodie's enigmatical features and opened the door.

A few steps inside, she entered a completely furnished living room with a beamed, acoustical ceiling. The starkness of the off-white walls and terrazzo floors was relieved by the greens, beiges and golds of contemporary pieces. The fireplace was framed by a gold sofa facing two easy chairs.

In the opposite corner of the room was a sweeping curved sofa in green tweed with armchairs in avocado and beige striped fabric. Emerald green lamps on matching end tables completed the arrangement. Despite the subtle elegance, every corner invited Jessica to sit down and relax.

But Brodie's hand at her elbow was guiding her to the formal dining room where a blue gray carpet accented the gold velvet of the chairs. The dining room credenza held a beautiful china set and figurines. Natural silk draperies hung at the windows.

From there it was on to a spacious U-shaped kitchen with blue-tile counters. Antique copper pieces decorated the wall. The room was complete with a breakfast nook — a cozy sitting room filled with white wicker.

Backtracking, Brodie showed her the den with its wall of books and pale brick fireplace. An area rug of chocolate brown complemented the beige plaid sofa and easy chairs that flanked the fireplace. A walnut desk dominated one side of the room.

The two guest bedrooms were skipped over as Brodie led her to the master bedroom. The king-size bed was covered with a white quilt. Cinnabar velvet upholstered two small armchairs arranged with a low table between them.

"What do you think?" Brodie finally broke the silence that had been between them.

"What can I say?" Jessica lifted her hands, at a loss for words. "It's beautiful!"

"Beautiful enough to live in?" he challenged. Jessica stared, hardly daring to believe what he was saying. Brodie continued before she could respond, "It's within easy reach of town yet far enough away to give us some privacy." Her heart sang at the pronounced, "I imagine you'll want to keep working, although I would much rather have you here waiting for me."

Jessica was so full of happiness she couldn't speak. But it didn't seem necessary. Somehow she found herself in his arms, her hands around his neck to bring his head down to hers. Their lips met in a fiery kiss that fused them together, golden flames shooting through her veins.

Higher and higher she was lifted on the cloud

of eternal joy. She clung to him, her life, her love. The dizzying climb was too much and she had to stop to catch her breath. She buried her face against his chest, feeling the roughness of his kisses on her hair. She was afraid she was going to do something silly like cry.

"Would it be very selfish of me," she murmured against his shirt, "to ask you to take a week off so we can have a honeymoon?"

Brodie became very still, his muscles tensing. "What honeymoon? What are you talking about, Jessica?" His hands gripped her shoulders to hold her away from him.

The smile faded from her lips as she stared at the puzzled frown above his hooded eyes. "Didn't you. . . . Didn't you just propose to me?" Her voice died to a whisper as she saw the answer in his face.

"No." The denial was flat and decisive. "I can't marry you, Jessica."

Letting her go, he walked several feet into the master bedroom and stopped to light a cigarette. His features seemed harsh and cruel in the wafting blue smoke. She felt drained and lifeless. The descent to earth had been too rapid.

"Why?" Her voice cracked and she tried to control it. "Do you already have a wife? Won't she give you a divorce? Is she sick or an invalid?" Now her voice sounded brittle, devoid of feeling.

"I have no wife," Brodie answered curtly.

"Marriage is out of the question."

"I see." Jessica thought she did see. Jordanna was the woman he wanted. If he couldn't marry her, he wasn't marrying anyone. "You want me to be your mistress."

"If you want to put it that way, yes." He blew out a stream of smoke with the words.

"Why bother with the house, then?" Her air of poise was thin, but it was holding. "Why not just ask me to quit my job and fly around the country with you?"

"I won't have you become a camp follower."

"But isn't that what a mistress is? Your own private —"

"I'm not going to get into a debate with you over definitions, Jessica," Brodie warned.

Her gaze fell beneath the icy blast of his. Her eyes ran sightlessly over the intricate pattern of the Oriental rug, as if searching for something but not knowing what.

"Have you made these convenient arrangements in other cities?" she questioned stiffly. "Memphis? Nashville?"

"No," he denied that, coming to stand in front of her. "I admit that I've had other women. But you're the only woman I want on more than a casual basis."

"Will I . . . have to share you with others?" Jessica faltered on the question although her voice remained cool.

His gaze bored into her. "You haven't shared me with others almost since the day we met.

182

Which is why I can't wait any longer. We either begin now or we stop." A silence ensued that Jessica couldn't break. Finally Brodie turned away. "I'm going to the basement to see if they've installed the new furnace. Look around some more. If you don't like the place, we'll find another." He walked out of the room.

Jessica stared at the empty doorway. It had been an ultimatum he had issued. And he had assumed she would stay. But was he wrong? If he hadn't put it in such black and white terms, if he had made love to her instead, she wouldn't be going through all this soul-searching now. It would be an accomplished fact.

The question wasn't — did she love him, but — could she leave him? A surge of despair sent her into the room. She paused at the bed, her fingertips touching the white quilted coverlet. This would be the bed they would share, the room where they would wake up together.

She wandered to the long closet. Their clothes would hang inside. She slid open the louvered doors and found the closet wasn't completely empty. A single hanger held a lacy peignoir. The store tags were still on it to show it was brand new.

There was something premeditated about it hanging there, as if Brodie never expected them to leave the house tonight. Perhaps if she had opened the refrigerator or cupboards in the kitchen, she would have found them stocked with food.

The house was all furnished, waiting to be occupied. Jessica knew she could fill it with love, maybe only with her love. She closed her eyes and pictured Brodie. Opening them, she took the lacy green peignoir from the closet and laid it on the bed. Mechanically she stripped off her clothes and hung them in the closet. When the frothy material of the peignoir was against her skin, she walked to the mirror and used the hair brush from the vanity set to fluff her hair.

At the sound of Brodie's footsteps in the hallway, she turned. A tremor ran through her limbs, but she was motionless when he appeared in the doorway. Brodie stopped, his muscled chest expanding in a breath he held, and stared. His eyes darkened to a disturbing hue as they made a slow, raking sweep of her.

Just as slowly, he walked to stand in front of her, looking down, not touching her, not making a move toward her. Jessica felt her breathing become shallow, her heartbeat become rapid and erratic. His control was supreme. She realized he was waiting for her to speak and make the first move.

Hesitantly she rested her hands on his waist and felt his muscles constrict. Swaying toward him, she wondered if she had the voice to speak.

"I want to live with you, Brodie." It came out trembling and low, but it was said.

His arms moved, but not to hold her. His hands found the bow that fastened the silly nothing robe covering the frothy gown. Brodie untied and pushed it off her shoulders, down her arms where it slid off to fall to the floor.

Jessica was a quaking mass of nerves, her bare feet as cold as ice, when Brodie swung her into his arms. He held her easily, as if she weighed no more than a feather. The bulging muscles of his arms formed an iron-hard cradle. His gaze never left her face as he carried her to the bed and laid her down as gently as a baby. He followed her down, stretching beside her, his hand cupping the side of her neck to feel the pulse that throbbed wildly there.

"I'll make you happy, Jessica." He smoothed the blond hair from her throat and kissed her leaping pulse.

Yes, she thought, temporarily he would make her ecstatically happy. Her hands slid inside the collar of his shirt. He tugged it free of the waistband of his pants and dispensed with the last few buttons, giving her free access to his warm, hard flesh.

His caressing hands explored her shoulders and arms and the hollows of her throat, ignoring the intimate areas covered by her flimsy gown as his mouth ignored the taste of her lips. Jessica begged him with her hands and lips and her body to make love to her.

"There's no need to rush, Green Eyes," he told her. "We've got all the time in the world now. And I'm going to use every damned minute of it."

Finally he ended the torment of her lips, covering them with a possessive kiss that gave her back a measure of reassurance. Jessica strained closer to his length, trying to absorb some of the strength he had in such abundance.

"Maybe I will take a few days off," Brodie nuzzled her ear. "I'm going to enjoy teaching you how to please me as much as I'm going to enjoy pleasing you."

A tiny sob came from her throat, born not out of desire but of pain, a pain of the heart. She tried to respond to his kisses, to unleash the love that consumed her. His hands now sought out her hips and waist and breasts, their irritation for the filmy gown growing in direct proportion to the increase of his carnal longing.

How many times he had wakened the same feelings in her! But this time something was wrong. The purity of her emotion had become tainted. What once she had given freely, she now held back, protecting and shielding.

"Green Eyes," he had called her. Was it really his pet name for her? Or did it belong to Jordanna? How many times would he hold her in his arms while she wondered if he was making love to her or pretending she was Jordanna? In the end, these doubts would destroy her love for him, and they would destroy her.

"No." It was the first word she had muttered since the agreement. It came out choked and broken. Brodie paid no attention to the negative sound until Jessica repeated it more forcefully, "No!" and began to struggle.

"What's the matter?" he frowned. "Have I hurt you? How?"

He had levered himself on his elbows above her. His shirt hung open, revealing tanned skin and a mass of curling dark hairs that veed to his stomach. Jessica closed her eyes, because she couldn't look at him without loving him.

"I — can't," she cried softly. "I can't go through with it!"

She attempted to roll away. "No!" Brodie's anger exploded. The iron hook of his arm caught her waist and tossed her back onto the mattress beside him. His legs covered hers to hold her there, pinning her with his weight. "You can't go this far and stop! My God, do you think I'm made of ice!" Imprisoning her arms, he spread-eagled them above her head.

Jessica stopped struggling. She kept her head averted, burying a cheek in the coverlet. Her breasts were rising and falling in deep, panicked breaths. Her eyes were tightly closed, one tear squeezing through her lashes.

"I can't, Brodie," she whispered. "I tried, but I can't."

And she waited for the final violence to erupt, knowing she had brought it on with her actions and prepared to pay for the mistake. She could hear Brodie's heavy breathing, disturbed by passion and anger. She waited for the punishment of his mouth, aware of the pressing heat of his body holding her down.

Instead she felt his weight ease from her. The creak of the bed springs was followed by the sound of his feet on the floor. Swallowing convulsively, she opened her eyes and slowly drew her arms to wrap them across her breasts, barely covered by the revealing garment. Brodie stood beside the bed watching her movements and noting the fearlike pain in her eyes.

His mouth had thinned into a cruel line, his features harshly condemning. Shards of blue steel filtered little of the chilling temperature of his gaze. Lust had gone from his expression, to be replaced by contempt.

Jessica dragged herself up, sliding to the opposite side of the bed. "I'm sorry, Brodie." He would never know how sorry she was.

"That's it, then." His voice was clipped and final. "It's over."

With heavy steps, she walked to the closet and took out her clothes. She hugged them to the thinness of her gown. The pain inside her was so intense, she wanted to die.

"Will you take me home, please?" she whispered.

There was a long silence. She thought for a minute he wasn't going to answer, then it came.

"Five minutes." It was a harsh, savage answer. "Be dressed and in the car." He issued the last as he was striding from the room.

Jessica was dressed in less than that. She paused at the door to wipe the single tear from her cheek, then hurried outside to the waiting car. The engine was running as she slid into the passenger seat.

Brodie never looked at her as he reversed out of the driveway. The envelope that had contained the key was still lying on the seat near her. Jessica slipped the key inside and returned the envelope to the glove compartment. She would never have a need for it.

She glanced at Brodie. His profile was almost savagely expressionless. Not once during the drive to her apartment did his gaze stray to her. It was as if he was the only one in the car. When he stopped in front of her building, Jessica hesitated, wanting to say something, but his hands remained on the steering wheel, the car idling. He stared straight ahead.

Finally Jessica opened the car door and climbed out. She had barely closed the door before Brodie was driving away. He had meant it. It was over and he had just cut her out of his life, ignoring her as if she didn't exist.

Chapter Twelve

With her arms hugging her knees, Jessica rocked gently on the sofa. It had been three weeks since Brodie had let her out in front of her apartment; three painful, heartrending weeks. She had lost weight and the dark shadows beneath her eyes revealed her incapacity for sleep.

Over and over again she went over the events. What had she hoped to gain? Had she thought if she denied Brodie the act of love that he would want her so badly he would offer marriage? If that had been her subconscious plan, it had backfired with agonizing consequences.

The telephone rang, and Jessica covered her ears with her hands. There wasn't anyone she wanted to talk to. She'd had more than enough advice to last her a lifetime. Between the receptionist, Ann, issuing platitudes and her uncle using anger to try to snap her out of her depression, she had been besieged with pearls of wisdom. They weren't any more comforting than the impersonal strand of pearls Brodie had given her. Everyone she knew had made some comment until she longed to lock herself in the apartment and never come out.

The telephone was insistent, ringing shrilly on the table beside the sofa. Jessica ignored it for as long as she could, then on the seventh ring, she reached for the receiver.

"Hello." Her voice was dull and lifeless. No one answered her, but she sensed there was someone on the other end of the line. "Hello?" she demanded with irritation.

"Who is that?" a voice snapped.

"It's Jessica Thor—" Then the quick, harsh voice heard so briefly, gripped her heart. "Brodie?" she whispered, clutching the receiver with both hands as if to hold onto him and never let him go.

"Sorry. I dialed this number by mistake." The voice never acknowledged his identity, but Jessica knew him just as she would know her own name.

"Brodie, please!" But the buzz of the dial tone was the only thing to hear her plea.

For long minutes she held onto the receiver. Hanging it up seemed to mean breaking some vital link. One tear rolled from her eyes, followed by a second and a third. When she put the phone down, an ocean of salty tears was drowning her cheeks. It was the first time she had truly cried. A stray tear here and there didn't really count. It took her all night to make up for the omission.

Perspiration stung her eyes. The cotton blouse she wore clung to her sticky skin. Summer had arrived in earnest, complete with heat and humidity. She used a folder as a fan, trying to stir the dead air of her closed-in office, but its relief was only temporary.

Impatiently she rose from her desk and walked into the reception area. "Ann, I can't stand much more of this. When is that man going to come and fix the air conditioner? That office is like a furnace!"

"He promised to be here by noon," the receptionist answered.

Jessica glanced at her watch. "He isn't late, is he?" she retorted sarcastically. "It's twenty to twelve."

"Do you suppose I should call him again?" Ann cast an uncertain glance at Jessica.

"Yes, you call him and you tell him that if he isn't over here by noon, he —" Her voice had grown steadily louder as her impatience had given way to anger.

A male voice interrupted, "He'd better be here this afternoon." Her threat was finished by her uncle. "You're getting a little hot under the collar, aren't you, Jessie?" Her uncle laughed at the pun he made.

"Very funny!" Jessica snapped, not at all amused.

"Where's your sense of humor, Jessie?" he admonished with a clicking tongue.

"It melted — in my office. I'm going to have one of the boys paint me a sign to hang on the door, identifying it for what it really is — a sweatbox," she insisted, and Ralph Dane laughed, which didn't improve her temper. "It's all very well for you to laugh. You have an enormous electric fan in your office."

"Naturally. It's my company," he smiled.

Suddenly Jessica was very close to tears. "Well, you can take your company and your fan and your sweatbox and you can —"

"Careful, careful, my dear." He was instantly at her side, his voice soothing her, a comforting arm curving around her shoulders. "I diagnose a severe case of heat exhaustion. My recommendation is that you have lunch in a cool, air-conditioned restaurant, preferably in the company of some handsome, distinguished man — namely me."

Jessica had succeeded in blinking back the tears and swallowing the anger. Now she laughed, somewhat tremulously. "If you think I'm going to refuse, you're wrong. I have a witness to that luncheon invitation, so you can't back out."

"I wouldn't dream of it." Her uncle turned to the receptionist. "If anyone wants to know where I am, tell them I'm lunching with a beautiful blonde. Unless my wife calls. Tell her I'm lunching with Jessie."

"Let me get my bag." Jessica dashed into her office and was out just as quickly.

Linking arms with her uncle, she walked out of the door with him. On the street, he guided her to his car and helped her into the passenger seat.

"Where would you like to go?" he asked,

sliding behind the wheel.

"I don't care, just as long as it's air-conditioned." Jessica rolled down the window to let the wind that was generated by the moving car blow over her face.

"I'm really proud of you, Jessica."

Both his statement and his use of her full name drew her attention from the passing scenery. "You are? I don't recall doing anything spectacular in the past week to earn such praise."

"I wasn't referring to the office. I meant that I'm proud of the way you managed to pull yourself together. A couple of months ago 1 would have sworn you were headed for a break-down," her uncle said.

Intense pain flashed across her face. She looked quickly out of the window, pressing a hand to her mouth to hide her trembling chin. Any unexpected reference to Brodie could crack her thin, protective shell.

"Time has a way of healing things," she lied. The wound was still bleeding.

"I know that's what people say, but we both know it isn't entirely true. I was rough on you a few times, but I was really only doing it for your own good. I apologize if you thought I was being heartless."

"I know you were, and I appreciated all your attempts," Jessica assured him, although she remembered one that had been particularly painful.

Looking back, she could see that she had failed miserably at her job the two months after she and Brodie had broken up. One morning her uncle had summoned her to his office and told her that she was to patch up whatever quarrel she'd had with Brodie. Since she had never given him the reason they had parted, she had been paralyzed by his order. When she had stared at him dumbstruck, he had changed his statement. He had told her that she had two choices — either patch things up or accept that it was over.

It was a painful memory, but it had proved to be the best advice she had received. It drummed in her mind every time she found herself dissolving in self-pity. She still hurt, but she had learned to live with it and conceal it from others.

"Here we are," her uncle announced.

Jessica pulled herself out of her recollections to see their destination. God, no, her heart cried in pain. It was the Terminal Station where Brodie had taken her for lunch. Her first impulse was to ask her uncle to take her else-where, but common sense overruled it. She couldn't keep avoiding places simply because she had been there with Brodie.

Hadn't she learned to walk the sidewalks and stop wondering when and if she would ever see him? Hadn't she learned not to look at the drivers of every expensive car, wondering if Brodie was in town?

Still her legs were shaking when she climbed out of the car and walked with her uncle to the renovated railroad station and the restaurant inside. Her smile to the hostess was tense as they were led through the tables to an empty one.

"Ralph!" a voice called to her uncle. "Hello, how are you?"

A man rose from a table near the window to greet them. It took Jessica only a second to recognize the bushy-browed man as Cal Janson. She had arranged to be busy the rare times he had stopped at the office on business. Mostly someone from the company went to see him.

"Hello, Cal. How's business?" Her uncle's hand was engulfed in a vigorous handshake.

"Fine, fine," Cal Janson replied, and turned his attention to her. "Jessica, you're looking more beautiful every time I see you." He clasped her hand warmly in both of his.

"Thank you." Inside she was praying frantically, *Please God, please, don't let him mention Brodie!*

"You make me wish I were ten years younger — well, maybe twenty," he winked at her uncle when he made the correction. "I was going to suggest to Brodie that the two of you come over to dinner tonight." It took all of Jessica's control not to blanch at his statement. It meant that Brodie was in town, and she didn't want to know that. "Since you're here, I'll extend the invitation to you first. Emily and I would love to have you."

"Thank you, but I'm afraid that isn't possible." Jessica was trying very hard to find a tactful way of telling Janson that she was no longer seeing Brodie.

He misunderstood her gentle wording. "That's why I'm asking you first. Brodie is very much his own master. I understand very well that he wants you all to himself, but if anyone can persuade him to accept the invitation, you can."

"But —"

"Here he comes now. We'll both go to work on him," Cal Janson declared, casting her a conspiratorial smile before directing his attention behind her.

Her heart stopped beating and her face drained of color as she pivoted. It was Brodie, purposefully winding his way through the tables to the windows. Tall, imposing, turning heads, he was more sternly handsome than she remembered. Devil-black hair, tanned skin stretched across cheekbones and jaw, the cruel line of his mouth, those piercing cold eyes, and that lobolike grace of movement, all struck her like a body blow, taking away her breath.

She wasn't ready to see him again. She wasn't prepared. Why did he have to show up just when she was beginning to put her life back together? She wanted to run, but she couldn't tear her eyes away from him.

What was he thinking right now? What was

he feeling? She searched his compelling features for a sign of reaction. There wasn't anything, just hard, cold stone. Surely he had seen her? He was looking right at her. Pain constricted her chest as Jessica realized he was looking *through* her.

"Hello, Brodie," Cal Janson greeted him. "Look who I ran into —"

"Hello, Cal." Brodie walked past her as if she weren't even there. "Sorry we're late. We were held up on the ground in Baltimore."

"I haven't been waiting long." Cal Janson darted a puzzled glance from Brodie to Jessica, her green eyes rounded with hurt, still staring at Brodie in disbelief. "I was just saying to Jessica that —"

"Drew and I had a chance to go over the latest balance sheet on the flight here," Brodie interrupted again. Jessica was only dimly conscious of the second man accompanying Brodie. Shock was still quaking through her as Brodie sat down at the table Janson had been given. He was ignoring the reference to her, treating her as if she didn't exist. "I didn't like the production figures. What's the problem? Are you having labor trouble?"

She was unaware of the frowning looks of confusion Brodie was receiving from both Drew and Cal Janson. Neither did she notice the indignant expression on her uncle's face. Hurt, humiliation and anger were all violently swelling up inside her. She wouldn't be snubbed this way.

Instinct and the desire to strike back directed her action. A glass of ice water was sitting on the table. Jessica picked it up and emptied it in Brodie's face. She didn't wait to see the results. Spinning away, she heard the muffled swearing and the gasps from onlookers. The only thing she wanted to do was get away from him as far and as fast as she could. Surprisingly her legs carried her swiftly over the winding path through the tables to the exit. Heads turned at the hastiness of her retreat, voices murmuring curiously.

The end of the long tunnel of pain and humiliation didn't seem very far away until a steel hand clamped itself on her arm and pulled her away. Just as savagely, it yanked her around and Jessica found herself facing Brodie. Moisture was beaded on his features, taut with rage. His brutal grip was threatening to break the bones in her arms.

"Let me go!" she hissed.

"Shut up!" His lip curled in a snarl, baring teeth in a wolflike display of anger.

Jessica strained against his hold, but didn't struggle. "Let me go or I'll have the manager call the police," she threatened in a treacherously low voice. Part of her couldn't help cowering from the savage fury in his eyes.

His answer was to jerk her onto tiptoes and silence her with the bruising force of his mouth. It deadened not only her voice but her will to fight. Her mind was all messed up by the sensations crowding in. She couldn't feel anything but the tautness of his muscled thighs and the solidness of his chest and the hard punishment of his mouth.

In the next second Brodie ended the kiss as abruptly as he had started it. Bereft, Jessica waited for whatever was to come next. Turning her, he pushed her toward the exit, not relinquishing his hold. They were nearly there when he was stopped.

"Brodie, for God's sake, what are you doing?" Drew was there, his face darkened with angry concern.

"Butt out!" Brodie snarled, and tried to shoulder his way past the attorney, but Drew was having none of it.

"Dammit, what's got into you? You deserved that ice water. My God, you can't treat people like that!" Drew flashed a worried look at Jessica. "Let go of her!"

"I said get out of my way!"

"Get out,'" Drew repeated, anger flashing in his eyes. "How far out do you want me to get? Maybe completely? Do you want my resignation? Is that what you've been pushing me to these past few months?"

"Frankly, Drew, I don't give a damn." This time Brodie physically pushed him out of the way and pulled Jessica along with him out the door.

"Where are we going?" Jessica was practically running in order to keep up with his long strides.

Her demand was met with the same response as previous ones, "Shut up!"

He continued to drag her along to the car. Opening the door, he pushed her inside and slammed it shut. Jessica rubbed her arm where his hard grip had bruised the flesh. Already the red marks had a bluish tinge to them. Excitement was mixed with fear at the way he had manhandled her into coming with him.

Intimidated by his rage now under slender control, Jessica sat quietly in her seat as Brodie drove out of the parking lot. She didn't reissue the question regarding their destination. Soon she guessed where it would be — her apartment.

Parked in front of the building, Brodie walked around to the passenger door, opened it and hauled her out without giving her a chance to step out on her own. Jessica bit her lip to check a protest of her treatment and let him push her inside. At the door, he ripped the key out of her hand, unlocked the door and shoved her inside.

With familiar ground beneath her feet, Jessica took a stand, facing him, a scant three feet separating them. "What comes next, Brodie? Rape?" Bravado trembled in her challenge.

His jaw tightened ominously. He turned

away, combing his fingers through his hair in a savage motion. "Damn you, Jessica," he muttered.

"Damn me?" An incredulous laugh ended in a sob. "Damn you for ignoring me as if I wasn't even there!"

The words were barely out before his fingers circled her throat. "It was either ignore you or kill you." The look in his eyes told her she should be terrified, but she couldn't bring herself to be afraid of him. "I could kill you for what you've done to me," Brodie said almost thoughtfully, his fingers tightening around her neck, interfering with her breathing. "Kill you and then myself. I'd be better off dead."

"Why?" His choking grip would only permit the one word.

"I've tried to forget you, crush all the memories, block out the smell and taste and feel of you, but I can't. The harder I try, the stronger they get, until — damn you!" he cursed. "And damn your memories for tormenting me with wanting you!"

His mouth came down hard and angry on her lips, punishing their softness. Behind the brutal possession, Jessica felt the pent-up agony of desire, the needing and wanting that she felt just as intensely. It was to this that she responded. The hand at her throat circled her neck while his arms crushed her to his length.

Hungrily his mouth moved to reexplore her face, not leaving an inch of it untouched.

Jessica clung to him, shaken by the fierceness of his desire.

"Is it really me you want?" she whispered.

"My God," Brodie breathed savagely. "There hasn't been anyone else since I met you. You've stolen my potency as well as my heart."

"What!" She tried to struggle away. His rough embrace had her senses clamoring so loudly that she couldn't hear her own thoughts. It was suddenly very necessary to be able to think and assimilate words.

He caught her face in his hands, holding it still, the blazing fire of his eyes smoldering over her features. "You're a heartless bitch. You'll give back neither my heart, my love nor my manhood."

"Brodie, do you love me?" Her voice throbbed. "Do you really love me?"

"Don't pretend you didn't know!" he jeered cruelly. "I spent more hours in the air just to see you than I ever did on any project. A man doesn't do that for mere lust."

"But I thought — Jordanna. . . ." Jessica was so confused that she didn't know what she thought.

"Your sister?" Brodie frowned as if incredulous that Jordanna had anything to do with their discussion.

"I thought you only wanted me because of her," she offered lamely.

"You mean because I was infatuated with her a long time ago?" he demanded.

"You did say I reminded you of her," Jessica defended. "When you. . . . That evening she was here, you hardly took your eyes off of her," she accused.

"That night I was so painfully conscious that you didn't want me there, I don't know where I was looking. If it was at Jordanna, I was probably trying to discover what I ever saw in her," Brodie retorted angrily before a frown of confusion flickered across his forehead. "Were you jealous that night?"

"Insanely jealous," she admitted with a faint laugh.

"My God!" he breathed. "And I thought . . . you believed I wasn't good enough to associate with your family."

"Brodie, no!" Jessica denied it vehemently, her fingers curving tightly over his wrists. "How could you possibly think that?"

His mouth twisted in a self-deprecating smile. "A lingering inferiority complex of the boy from the wrong side of town. As for Jordanna, initially I was interested in dating you because of her. The prospect of going to bed with you satisfied a longing to avenge that previous rejection by a Thorne. But after the third or fourth time I saw you, the sensations you were arousing in me had nothing to do with vengeance."

Of its own volition, her body molded itself to the hard length of his, her heart thrilling to his declaration. "I love you, Brodie," she responded, trembling with the depth of her emotion.

His arms encircled her in an iron band of love that crushed her to him, as if he was intent on defying the physical restrictions of their bodies to bring her closer to him still. His mouth moved roughly over her hair, kissing and caressing.

"If you love me, why did you put us through this hell?" Brodie demanded, his voice echoing the shudder that racked through him. "Why did you refuse to come to me?"

"Because . . . I think I hoped if I wouldn't let you make love to me, you'd marry me," Jessica admitted. "I wanted to be your wife, Brodie. I wanted to share your life, not just your bed."

"You'll get your wish," he told her grudgingly. "If that's the only way I can have you, then I'll marry you."

"Why, Brodie?" She drew her head away from his to gaze in confusion at his face. "*Why* don't you want to marry me?"

"Because — just look around you. You have everything. You've always had everything — clothes, the finest schools, a beautiful home. Everything you've ever wanted." Impatience darkened his eyes.

"Money? That's your reason?" Jessica frowned. "What difference should that make to you? You're wealthy and successful. As a matter of fact, you were intent on keeping me in a style I wasn't accustomed to."

"Yes, I have money today," he snapped. "But I'm not a blind fool. I can't expect to come up a winner every time I roll the dice. I could lose everything I have tomorrow."

"Money doesn't mean anything to me. I don't care whether you have any or not. I love you," she argued.

"Noble words," Brodie jeered with contempt. "But you don't know what it can be like to have nothing. When that day of cold reality comes, you'll find that love isn't enough."

"It is!" Jessica searched for a way to prove to him that it was true. "It isn't everything, but it's enough. These past few months we've been apart, I've had all those expensive gifts you gave me, but they didn't mean anything because I didn't have you. You said it yourself, Brodie — what value is money if you can't share it with the one you care about? Without money, you can still share your love with that person."

She would have continued, but Brodie was convinced. He silenced her in a most satisfying way.